DEATH OF A NAG

A Hamish Macbeth Murder Mystery

M. C. Beaton

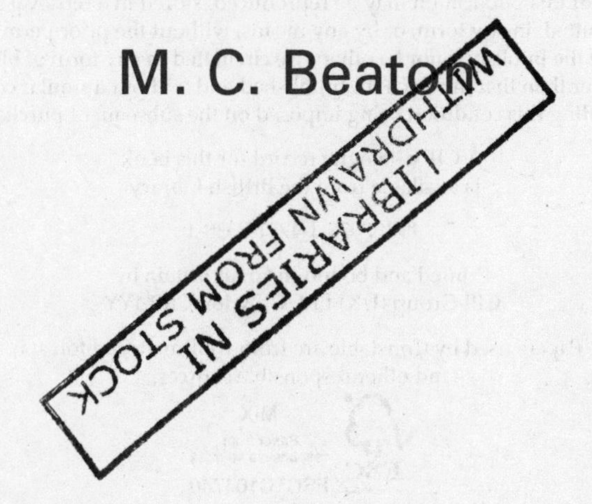

Constable • London

CONSTABLE

First published in the USA by The Mysterious Press,
Warner Books, Inc., 1995

First published in the UK by Robinson,
an imprint of Constable & Robinson Ltd., 2009

This edition published by C&R Crime,
an imprint of Constable & Robinson Ltd., 2013

Reprinted in 2016 by Constable

5 7 9 10 8 6 4

A CIP catalogue record for this book
is available from the British Library.

ISBN 978-1-4721-0530-1

Printed and bound in Great Britain by
CPI Group (UK) Ltd, Croydon CR0 4YY

Papers used by Constable are from well-managed forests
and other responsible sources.

Constable
is an imprint of
Little, Brown Book Group
Carmelite House
50 Victoria Embankment
London EC4Y 0DZ

An Hachette UK Company
www.hachette.co.uk

www.littlebrown.co.uk

Hamish Macbeth fans share their reviews . . .

'Treat yourself to an adventure in the Highlands; remember your coffee and scones – for you'll want to stay a while!'

'I do believe I am in love with Hamish.'

'M. C. Beaton's stories are absolutely excellent . . . Hamish is a pure delight!'

'A highly entertaining read that will have me hunting out the others in the series.'

'A new Hamish Macbeth novel is always a treat.'

'Once I read the first mystery I was hooked . . . I love her characters.'

Share your own reviews and comments at www.constablerobinson.com

Chapter One

O the disgrace of it! –
The scandal, the incredible come-down!
– Sir Max Beerbohm

Hamish Macbeth awoke to another day. His dog, Towser, was lying across his feet, snoring rhythmically. Sunlight slanted through the gap in the curtains. The telephone in the police office part of the house shrilled and then the answering machine clicked on. He should rise and go and find out what it was. It was his duty as a police constable of the village of Lochdubh and part of the surrounding area of the county of Sutherland. But all he wanted to do was pull the duvet over his head and go back to sleep.

He could not really think of any good reason for getting up to face the day.

He had, until his demotion from sergeant back to constable and the end of his engagement with Priscilla Halburton-Smythe, daughter of a local hotelier, been very popular, a happy state of affairs he had taken for granted. But somehow the story had got about that he had cruelly jilted Priscilla, she who had been too good for him in the first place, and so, when he went about his duties, he was met with reproachful looks. Although Chief Superintendent Peter Daviot had also been angry with him over the end of the engagement, that was not why Hamish had been demoted. He had solved a murder mystery by producing what he firmly believed was the body of the murdered man to elicit a shock confession from the guilty party. The ruse had worked, but he had had the wrong body. It had turned out to be a fine example of Pictish man and the police were accused of being clod-hopping morons for having so roughly handled and used such a prime exhibit. Someone had to be punished, and naturally that someone was Hamish Macbeth.

Hamish was not an ambitious man. In fact, he was quite happy with his lot as an ordinary police constable, but he felt the displeasure of the village people keenly. His days before his disgrace had pleasantly been given up to mooching around the village and gossiping. Now no one seemed to want to spend the time of day with him, or that was the way it seemed to his gloomy mind. If Priscilla, whom Hamish considered remarkably unaffected by the end to the romance, had stayed around to demonstrate that fact, then he would not be in bad odour. But she had left to stay with friends in Gloucestershire for an extended visit, so as far as the villagers were concerned, Hamish had driven her off and she was down in 'foreign' parts, nursing a broken heart.

Mrs Halburton-Smythe did not help matters by shaking her head and murmuring 'Poor Priscilla' whenever Hamish's name was mentioned, although what Mrs Halburton-Smythe was sad about was that she was beginning to believe that her cool and aloof daughter did not want to marry anyone.

With a groan, Hamish made the effort and got up. Towser gave a grumbling sound in the back of his throat and slid to the floor and padded off towards the kitchen.

Hamish jerked back the curtains. The police station was on the waterfront and overlooked the sea loch, which lay that morning as calm as a sheet of glass.

He washed and dressed and went through to the police office. The message was from headquarters in Strathbane reminding him he had not sent in a full statement about a break-in at a small hotel on the road to Drim. He ambled into the kitchen and made himself a breakfast of bread and cheese, for he had forgotten to light the stove. Priscilla had presented him with a brand-new electric cooker, but he had childishly sent it back.

He fed Towser and stood on one leg, irresolute, looking like a heron brooding over a pond. Depression was new to him. He had to take action, to do something to lift it. He could start by typing that report. On the other hand, Towser needed a walk.

The phone began to ring again and so he quickly left the police station with Towser at his heels and set out along the waterfront in the hot morning sun. And it was hot, a most unusual state of affairs for the north of Scotland. He pushed his peaked cap back on his fiery-red hair and his hazel eyes saw irritation heading his way in the form of the Currie sisters, Jessie and Nessie.

The eyes of the village spinsters constantly accused him of being a heartless flirt. He touched his cap and said, 'Fine morning.'

'It is for some. It is for some,' said Jessie, who had an irritating habit of repeating things. 'Some, on the other hand, are breaking their hearts.'

Hamish skirted round them and went on his way. Resentment and self-pity warred in his bosom. He had once helped the Currie sisters out of a dangerous jam and had destroyed evidence to do so. Damn it, he had helped a lot of people in this village. Why should he be made to feel guilty?

His thoughts turned to Angela Brodie, the doctor's wife. Now *she* had not turned against him. He walked up the short path leading to the doctor's house, went round the back and knocked at the kitchen door. Angela answered it, the dogs yapping at her feet. She pushed her fine wispy hair out of her eyes and said vaguely, 'Hamish! How nice. Come in and have coffee.'

She cleared a space for him at the kitchen table by lifting piles of books off it and placing them on the floor.

'I don't seem to have had a chat with you in ages,' said Angela cheerfully. 'Heard from Priscilla?'

Hamish, who had just been lowering his bottom on to a kitchen chair, stood up again. 'If you are going to start as well . . .' he began huffily.

'Sit down,' said Angela, startled. 'Start what?'

Hamish slowly sat down again. 'You haff been the only one who hass not gone on about Priscilla,' he said, his Highland accent becoming more sibilant, as it always did when he was angry or upset.

'Oh, I see,' said Angela, pouring him a mug of coffee and sliding it across the table towards him. 'I only asked about Priscilla because I assumed that you and she were still friends.'

'And so we are!' said Hamish. 'But ye wouldnae think so with this lot in Lochdubh. You would think I wass some sort of Victorian philanderer the way they go on.'

'It'll blow over,' said Angela comfortably. 'These sort of ideas spread through these villages like an infection. Mrs Wellington started it.' Mrs Wellington was the minister's wife. 'She started it by complaining that you were a feckless womanizer and things like that. You know how she goes on. But you brought that on yourself!'

'How?'

'She happened to overhear you doing a very good impression of her to delight the boy scouts.'

'Ah.'

'And so she got a resentment to you and shared it around. Resentment is very infectious. It has always fascinated me the way, for example, one malcontent can bring a whole factory out on strike and keep everyone out on strike until the firm folds and they all lose their jobs. Also, you're going around being so gloomy. That fuels it. You look like a guilty man.'

'I'm a bit down,' confessed Hamish. 'The fact is I've taken a scunner tae Lockdubh and everyone in it.'

'Hamish! You love the place!'

'Not at the moment.'

'You're due some leave, aren't you? Get right away on holiday. You could get one of those cheap holidays in Spain. Or some of the African package holidays are very cheap.'

'I'll think about it,' said Hamish moodily. 'I might just take a wee holiday somewhere in Scotland, seeing that the weather's fine.'

Angela got up and began to rummage through a pile of old magazines on a kitchen chair. She extracted a battered Sunday paper colour supplement. 'What about this place?' she said, flipping open the pages. 'Skag. Have you been to Skag?'

'That's over on the Moray Firth. I havenae been there, though I've been into Forres, which is quite close.' He looked at the coloured photographs. It looked like a Cornish resort with long white beaches, pretty village and harbour. There was also a page of advertisements for hotels and boarding-houses in Skag. 'I'll take this with me, Angela, if you don't mind.'

'Keep it,' said the doctor's wife. 'It's one less piece of junk. I can never bring myself to throw magazines out or even take them along to the waiting-room.'

'What's the latest gossip?' asked Hamish.

She sipped her coffee and looked at him in that vague way she always had. Then she put down her coffee-cup and said, 'Well, the biggest piece of gossip apart from yourself is Jessie Currie.'

'What about her?'

'Angus Macdonald, the seer, told her she would be married before the year's out.'

Hamish's hazel eyes lit up with amusement. 'She didnae believe him, did she?'

'She says she didn't, but she's been casting a speculative eye over the men of the village and Nessie is worrying about being left alone.'

'And who is this charmer who's going to sweep our Jessie off her feet?'

'Angus will only say it's going to be a divorced fisherman.'

'We don't have any divorced fishermen!'

'I pointed that out to Jessie and she said, "Not yet."'

'Chance'll be a fine thing,' said Hamish. 'Dried-up old spinster like her.'

'Hamish! That's cruel.'

'Aye, well, she should mind her own business instead of ither folks'.'

'I really do think you need to get away. Willie Lamont was saying the other day that when you go to the restaurant, you're always complaining about something.'

Willie Lamont, Hamish's one-time sidekick, had left the police force to marry a young relative of the owner of the Italian restaurant and worked there much harder than he had ever done when he was a police constable.

'The portions are getting smaller and smaller and the prices higher.'

'Still, it's not like you to complain. I'll bet if you had a break from all of us, you'd be very happy to come back and see us again.'

Hamish got up. 'We'll see. Thanks for the coffee.'

He walked along the waterfront and perched on the harbour wall. Towser sighed and lay down. Hamish studied the magazine article. There was an advertisement from a boarding-house called The Friendly House 'situated right on the beach with commanding sea views, old-fashioned cooking; special low terms for July, halfboard.'

Hamish lowered the magazine and looked over at the village. It was a largely Georgian village, built all in the same year by one of the dukes of Sutherland to enlarge the fishing industry, trim little square whitewashed houses facing the sea loch. He knew everyone in the village, from people who had lived there all their lives like the Currie sisters, to the latest incomers. He felt better now he had talked to Angela, much better. He had been seeing things through a distorting glass, imagining everyone was against him.

So when he saw Mrs Maclean, Archie, the fisherman's wife, stumping along towards him, carrying a heavy shopping basket, he gave her a cheery smile. 'Lazing about as usual?' demanded Mrs Maclean. She was a ferocious housekeeper, never seen without a pinafore and smelling strongly of soap and disinfectant. Her hair was twisted up in foam rollers and covered with a headscarf.

'I am enjoying the day,' said Hamish mildly.

'How ye can enjoy anything wi' that poor lassie down in England eating her heart out is beyond me,' said Mrs Maclean.

Hamish studied her thoughtfully and then a gleam of malice came into his eyes. 'Priscilla isn't nursing a broken heart, but some poor fisherman's wife is soon going tae be.'

'Whit dae ye mean?'

Hamish slid down from the wall, rolled up the colour supplement and put it in his trousers pocket. 'Aye, Angus Macdonald told Jessie Currie she'd be married afore the year was out and tae a fisherman, a *divorced* fisherman. How's Archie these days?'

'Archie's jist fine,' said Mrs Maclean, her eyes roving this way and that, as if expecting to see her husband. It was well known in the village that Archie, when not fishing, spent most of the day avoiding his wife, in case she scrubbed him to death, as he put it. 'Anyway, it's all havers,' she said. 'Jessie Currie. The very idea.'

And then, to Hamish's delight, he saw Archie in the distance. He came abreast of the Curries' cottage and Jessie called something to him over the garden hedge and he stopped to talk to her.

'There's your man ower there,' said Hamish happily, 'and talking tae Jessie.'

Mrs Maclean stared in the direction he pointed and gave something that sounded like a yelp and set off at speed. But Archie saw her coming and left Jessie and darted up one of the lanes leading up to the back village and was gone from view.

Hamish strolled back to the police station, phoned Strathbane and said he wanted to take three weeks' immediate holiday. Permission was easily granted. The bane of his life, Detective Chief Inspector Blair, was in Glasgow. There had been virtually no crime at all for months, and so it was agreed that Sergeant Macgregor over at Cnothan could take over Hamish's duties as well as his own. He was free to leave at the end of the week. He phoned the boarding-house in Skag and learned to his delight that, thanks to a cancellation, they had one room free for the very time he wanted, and yes, dogs were allowed.

Feeling happier than he had felt for some time, he then set out to arrange for his sheep to be looked after, his hens and ducks as well, and then decided to pay a visit to the seer to find out what had possessed the old sinner to wind Jessie up like that.

Angus Macdonald, the seer, a big, craggy man like one of the minor prophets, peered all around Hamish looking for a present before he let him in. The villagers usually brought him something, a bottle of whisky or a cake.

'No, I didnae bring you anything,' said Hamish, following him into his small living room. 'I don't want your services. I simply want to know what you were doing telling Jessie she was going tae marry a divorced fisherman.'

'I seed it,' said Angus huffily. 'I dinnae make things up.'

'Come on, man. Jessie!'

'Well, that's whit I seed.'

'That sort o' rubbish could start gossip.'

'Maybe that's whit you're hoping fur, Hamish.'

'How's that?'

'Stop them gossiping about you and your lassie.'

'I think you're an old fraud,' said Hamish. 'I've always thought you were an old faker.'

'You're jist bad-tempered because ye think nobody loves ye. Here's Mrs Wellington coming.'

Hamish jumped up in alarm. He scampered off and ran down the hill, seemingly deaf to the booming hail of the minister's wife.

'That man,' said the tweedy Mrs Wellington as she plumped herself down in an armchair. 'I'll be glad to see the back of him.'

'Is he going somewhere?' asked Angus.

'I met Mrs Brodie just before I came up here. She said that Hamish was thinking of going over to Skag for a holiday.'

'Oh, aye,' said Angus. 'Now whit can I dae for you, Mrs Wellington?'

'This business about Jessie Currie. It can't be true.' Her eyes sharpened. 'Unless you've heard something.'

'I see things,' said Angus.

'And you hear more gossip than anyone I know,' said Mrs Wellington sharply. 'I brought you one of my fruitcakes. It's over on the counter. You see, Mr Patel at the stores told me that he had seen Archie Maclean talking to Jessie Currie and when he saw his wife at the other end of the waterfront coming towards him, he ran away.'

'I'm saying nothing,' said Angus mysteriously. 'But we'll jist have a wee cup o' tea and try that cake.'

Early on Saturday morning, Hamish Macbeth hung a sign on the door of the police station, referring all inquiries to Sergeant Macgregor at Cnothan. He locked the police Land Rover up in the garage, put Towser on the leash, and picked up his suitcase. Then the phone in the police station began to ring. He decided to answer it in the hope that someone in the village might have phoned up to wish him a happy holiday.

The voice of the seer sounded down the line. 'I wouldnae go tae Skag if I were you, Hamish.'

Hamish felt a superstitious feeling of dread. 'Why not?' he asked.

'I see death. I see death and trouble fur you, Hamish Macbeth.'

'I havenae time to listen to your rubbish,' said Hamish sharply and put the receiver down.

At the other end of the line, Angus listened to that click and smiled. Called him a fraud, had he? Well, that should give Hamish Macbeth something to think about!

Hamish left the police station and walked along to the end of the harbour to get the bus to Bonar Bridge. From Bonar Bridge he would get another bus to Inverness and then buses from Inverness over to Skag.

The bus was, as usual, late, twenty minutes late, in fact. Hamish was the only passenger. He often thought the driver, Peter Dunwiddy, deliberately started off late so as to have an excuse to break the speed limit, even with a policeman on board. Hamish hung on tightly and Towser flattened himself on the floor of the bus as it hurtled up out of Lochdubh and then began to scream around the hairpin bends on its way to Bonar Bridge. He expected to feel a lightness of heart as Lochdubh and all its residents fell away behind him. But he felt an odd tugging sadness at his heart. To match his mood, the day was grey, all colour bleached out of the landscape, like a Japanese print. He hoped the good weather would return. Perhaps he should not have been so parochial as to holiday in Scotland. When did Scotland ever guarantee sunny weather and water warm enough to go for a swim?

By the time he reached the village of Skag, he felt as tired as if he had walked there. He asked directions to The Friendly House and then set out. It was about two miles outside the village, and not on the beach exactly but behind a row of sand dunes set a quarter of a mile back from the North Sea.

It was an old Victorian villa, vaguely Swiss-chalet design, with fretted-wood balconies and blue shutters. He glanced at his watch. Half past five. Tea was at six.

He entered a dim hallway furnished with a side-table holding an assortment of tourist brochures, a large brass bowl holding dusty pampas-grass, a carved chair, and an assortment of wellington boots. He pressed a bell on the wall and a door at the back of the wall opened and a thick, heavyset man came towards him. He had blond hair and bright blue eyes and a skin which had a strange high glaze on it, like china. Hamish thought he was probably in his fifties.

'You must be our Mr Macbeth,' he said breezily. 'The name's Rogers, Harry Rogers. You'll find us one happy family here. Come upstairs and I'll show you and the doggie your room.'

The room boasted none of the modern luxuries like telephone or television. But the bed looked comfortable, and through the window Hamish could see the grey line of the North Sea. 'The bathroom's at the end of the corridor,' said Mr Rogers. 'As you see, there's a wash-hand basin in the corner there. Tea's at six. Yes, none of this dinner business. Good old-fashioned high tea.'

Hamish thanked him and Mr Rogers left. Towser, tired after the long walk, crawled on to the bed and closed his eyes. Hamish quickly unpacked, taking out a bowl which he filled with water for the dog, and a can of dog food, a can opener and another bowl. He filled the second bowl with the dog food and put it on the floor beside the water. Spoilt Towser did not like dog food, but, reflected Hamish, he would just need to put up with it for the duration of the holiday. Of course, maybe he could buy him some cold ham as a treat. Towser was partial to cold ham. He changed into a pair of jeans and a checked shirt, debated whether to wear a tie and decided against it, and then went downstairs and pushed open a door marked 'Dining Room'. A small, birdlike woman who turned out to be Mrs Rogers, hailed him. 'Mr Macbeth, your table's here . . . with Miss Gunnery.'

Hamish nodded to Miss Gunnery and sat down. All the other diners were already seated. Mr Rogers appeared and introduced everyone to everyone else. Hamish's quick policeman's mind noted all the names and his sharp eyes took in the appearance of the other guests.

Miss Gunnery on the other side of the table had the sort of appearance which even in these modern days screamed spinster. She had a severe face, gold-rimmed glasses and a mouth like a trap. Her flat-chested figure was dressed, despite the humidity of the day, in a green tweed suit worn over a white shirt blouse.

At the next table was a man with his wife, a Mr and Mrs Harris. Both were middle-aged. She had neatly permed brown hair and neat, closed features, and was dressed in a woollen sweater and cardigan and a black skirt. Her husband was wearing an open-necked shirt and a trendy black leather jacket and jeans, the sort of outfit that tired businessmen in a search for fading youth have taken to wearing, almost like a uniform. He was grey-haired, had large staring eyes and a bulbous nose.

Beyond them were Mr and Mrs Brett and their three children, Heather, Callum and Fiona, aged seven, four and three, respectively. Mr Brett was a comfortable, chubby man with glasses and an air of benign stupidity. His wife was an artificial redhead with a petty face and pencilled eyebrows. Either they were plucked, a rare fashion these days, thought Hamish, or they had fallen off, or she had been born that way. She had pencilled in arches of eyebrows, which gave her a look of perpetual surprise.

At the window table were two girls called Tracey Fink and Cheryl Gamble, both from Glasgow. They both had hair sunstreaked by chemicals rather than sunlight and white pinched faces under a load of make-up, and both were wearing identical outfits, striped black-and-white sweaters and black ski pants with straps under the instep and dirty sneakers. And in a far corner was a solitary man who had the honour of having a table to himself. His name was Mr Andrew Biggar. He had a tanned face and thick brown hair streaked with grey, small clever brown eyes, and a long, humorous mouth.

High tea, that famous Scottish meal now hardly ever served, consists of one main dish, usually cold ham, and salad and chips, washed down with tea. In the middle of each table was a cake stand. On the bottom were thin slices of white bread scraped with butter.

On the next layer were scones and teacakes, and on the top, cakes filled with ersatz cream and covered in violently-coloured icing.

'Grand day,' said Hamish conversationally to Miss Gunnery, for every day in Scotland where it is not exactly freezing cold and pouring wet is designated a 'grand day'.

Her eyes snapped at him through her glasses. 'Is it? I find it damp and overcast.'

Hamish relapsed into a crushed silence. He wished he had not come. But Mr Harris's voice rose above the conversation at the other tables, he of the trendy leather jacket, and caught Hamish's attention.

'Well, this holiday was your idea, Doris,' he said.

'I only said the tea was a trifle weak,' protested his wife.

'Always finding fault, that's your problem,' said Mr Harris. 'If you exercised more and thought less about your stomach, you might be as fit as me.'

'I only said –'

'You said. You said,' he jeered. He looked around the room. 'That's women for you. Always nit-picking.'

'Bob, *please,*' whispered his wife.

'Please what?'

'*You* know.' She cast a scared look around the dining room. 'Everyone's listening.'

'Let them listen. I'm not bound by your suburban little fears, my dear.' His voice rose to a high falsetto. 'What *will* the neighbours think.'

And so he went on and on.

The severe Miss Gunnery, who prided herself on 'keeping herself to herself', was driven to open her mouth and say to the tall, lanky, red-headed man opposite, 'That fellow is a nag.'

'Aye, the worst kind,' agreed Hamish, and then smiled, and at that smile, Miss Gunnery thawed even more. 'Mrs Harris is right,' she said. 'The tea is disgustingly weak, the ham is mostly fat, and those cakes look vile. I know this place is cheap . . .'

'Maybe there's a fish-and-chip shop in the village,' said Hamish hopefully. 'I might take a walk there later. My dog likes fish and chips.'

'Oh, you have a dog? What breed?'

'Towser's a mixture of every kind of breed.'

Miss Gunnery looked amused. 'Towser! I didn't think anyone called a dog Towser these days – or Rover, for that matter.'

'It started as a wee bit o' a joke, that name,' said Hamish, 'and then the poor animal got stuck wi' it.'

'What do you do for a living, Mr Macbeth?'

The nag's voice had temporarily ceased. There was silence in the dining room. 'I'm a civil servant,' said Hamish. He did not like telling people he was a policeman because they usually shrank away from him. And he had found that when he said he was a civil servant, it sounded so boring that no one ever asked him where he worked or in what branch of the organization.

'I'm a schoolteacher,' said Miss Gunnery. 'I've never been to Skag before. It seemed a good chance to get a cheap holiday.'

'When did you arrive?'

'Today, like the rest. We're all the new intake.'

Mr Rogers and his wife hovered about among the tables, snatching away plates as soon as any diner looked as if he or she was finished. 'We have television in the lounge across the hall,' announced Mr Rogers. His wife was carefully packing away uneaten cakes into a large plastic box. Hamish guessed, and as it turned out correctly, that they would make their appearance again during the following days until they had all either been eaten or gone stale.

The company moved through to the lounge. Bob Harris had temporarily given up baiting his wife, but Andrew Biggar made the mistake of asking Doris Harris what she would like to see.

'"Coronation Street" is just about to come on,' said Doris shyly. 'I would like to see that if no one else minds.'

Her husband's voice cut across the murmur of assent. 'Trust you to inflict your penchant for soaps on everyone else. How you can watch that pap is beyond me.'

Hamish walked over to the television set, found 'Coronation Street', and turned up the volume. 'I like "Coronation Street",' he lied to Doris. 'Always watch it.'

He sat down next to Miss Gunnery. He was aware of the nag's voice all through the programme, sneering and jeering at the characters. He sighed and looked about the room. The chairs were arranged in a half-circle in front of the television set. The fireplace was blocked up and a two-bar electric heater stood in front of it. There was a set of bookshelves containing battered paperbacks, no doubt left behind by previous guests. The Rogerses were probably too mean to buy any. The chairs were upholstered in a scratchy fabric. The carpet was a worn-out green with faded yellow flowers. There were various dim pictures on the walls, Highland cattle in Highland mist, and a grim photograph of a Victorian lady who stared down on all. Probably the original owner, thought Hamish.

At the end of the programme, which he had only stayed to watch for Mrs Harris's sake, he rose and said to Miss Gunnery, 'I'm going to walk my dog along to the village and see if there's a fish-and-chips shop. Want to come?'

'I don't eat fish and chips,' she said primly, looking down her nose.

The tetchiness that had been in him for months rose to the surface again. 'So you prefer that high-class muck we had for tea?'

There was an edge of contempt to his light Highland voice and Miss Gunnery flushed. 'I'm being silly,' she said, getting to her feet. 'I'd enjoy the walk.'

Hamish went up to get Towser, but when he descended to the hall again it was to find not only Miss Gunnery waiting for him but the rest of the party, with the exception of the Harrises.

They did not say anything like 'We've decided to come too,' but merely fell into line behind the policeman like obedient children being taken for a walk.

Mr Brett was the first to break the silence. 'A stone's throw from the sea,' he exclaimed. 'You would need to have a strong arm to throw a stone that distance.'

'Are ye sure there's a chip shop, Jimmy?' asked Cheryl. She hailed from Glasgow, where everyone was called Jimmy, or so it seemed, if you listened to the inhabitants.

'I don't know,' said Hamish. 'May be something in the pub.'

'I'm starving,' confided Tracey, stooping to pat Towser. 'I could eat a horse between two bread vans.'

Cheryl slapped her playfully on the back and both girls giggled.

'It's a pity little Mrs Harris couldn't come as well,' said Andrew Biggar. 'Don't suppose she gets much fun. Are you in the army, by any chance, Mr Macbeth?'

'Hamish. I'm called Hamish. No, Andrew. Civil servant. What makes ye say that?'

'When I first saw you, I thought you were probably usually in uniform. Got it wrong. I'm an army man myself. Forcibly retired.'

'Oh, those dreadful redundancies,' said Miss Gunnery sympathetically. 'And us so soon to be at war with Russia again.'

'Don't say that,' said Mrs Brett, whose name turned out to be June, and her husband's, Dermott. 'It's been a grim enough start. That man Harris should be shot.'

'You can say that again,' said Dermott Brett, so June predictably did and the couple roared with laughter at their own killing wit.

'I don't know if I'm going to be able to bear this holiday,' murmured Miss Gunnery to Hamish.

'Och,' said Hamish, who was beginning to feel better, 'I think they're a nice enough bunch of people and there's nothing like a common resentment for banding people together.' He winced remembering how common resentment had turned the villagers of Lochdubh against him.

'Harris, you mean,' said Miss Gunnery. 'But his voice does go on and on and it's not a very big place.'

They arrived at the village of Skag. It consisted of rows of stone houses, some of them thatched, built on a point. The river Skag ran on one side of the point and on the other side was the broad expanse of the North Sea. The main street was cobbled but the little side streets were not surfaced and the prevalent white sand blew everywhere, dancing in little eddies on a rising breeze. 'Getting fresher,' said Hamish. 'Look there. A bit of blue sky.'

They walked down to the harbour and stood at the edge. The tide was coming in and the water sucked greedily at the wooden piles underneath them. Great bunches of seaweed rose and fell. Above them, the grey canopy rolled back until bright sunlight blazed down.

Hamish sniffed the air. 'I smell fish and chips,' he said, 'coming from over there.'

They set out after him and found a small fish-and-chips shop. Hamish suggested they walk to the beach and eat their fish and chips there.

They made their way with their packets past the other side of the harbour, where yachts were moored in a small basin, the rising wind humming and thrumming in the shrouds. There was a sleazy café overlooking the yacht basin, still open but empty of customers, the lights of a fruit machine winking in the gloom inside.

A path led round the back of the café, past rusting abandoned cars and fridges, old sofas and broken tables, to a rise of shingle and then down to where the shingle ended and the long white beach began.

'You spoil that dog,' said Miss Gunnery as Hamish placed a fish supper on its cardboard tray down in front of Towser

Hamish did not reply. He knew he spoilt Towser but did not like anyone to comment on the fact.

'Why does a woman like Doris marry a pillock like that?' asked Andrew Biggar.

June Brett nudged her chubby husband playfully in the ribs. 'They're all saints before you marry them and then the beast comes out.'

Dermott Brett snarled at her and his wife shrieked with delight. Faces could be misleading, thought Hamish. June looked rather petty and mean when she was not speaking, but when she did, she became transformed into a good-natured woman. The Brett children were making sandcastles down by the water. They were remarkably well-behaved. Heather, the seven-year-old, was looking after her young brother and toddling sister, making sure that little Fiona did not wander into the water. Long ribbons of white sand snaked along the harder damp surface of the sand underneath and then there came a haunting humming sound, 'Whit's that?' cried Cheryl, clutching Tracey.

'Singing sands,' said Hamish. 'I remember hearing there were singing sands here but I forgot about it.'

'It's eerie,' said Miss Gunnery. 'In fact, the whole place is a bit odd. It never gets dark this time of year, does it, Hamish?'

He shook his head, thinking that the place was indeed eerie. Because of the bank of shingle behind the beach and the flatness of the land behind, there was a feeling of being cut off from the rest of the world. He remembered the seer's prediction with a shudder and then his common sense took over. Angus had heard the gossip about his holiday and had invented death and trouble to pay Hamish back for having called him a fraud.

Miss Gunnery was carefully collecting everyone's fish-and-chip papers when Hamish heard Dermott Brett say, 'He's got worse.'

'Who?' asked Andrew, lazily scraping in the sand for shells.

'Bob Harris.'

'You know him? Asked Hamish.

'Yes, he was here last year.'

Miss Gunnery paused in her paper-gathering. 'You mean you stayed here and *came back*!'

'New management,' said Dermott Brett. 'It was owned by a couple of old biddies. They did a good tea, but their prices were quite high for a boarding-house. We weren't going to come back, because with the three kids it was coming to quite a bit. Then June saw the ad with the new cheap prices, but it said nothing about new management.'

'What happened to the old women who owned it?' asked Hamish, ever curious.

'They were the Blane sisters, the Misses Blane. Rogers said they took a small house for themselves in Skag. Might call on them, if I can find them.'

'So Harris is worse now?' pursued Hamish.

'He was bad enough last year, but in fits and starts. Didn't go on like he does now the whole time. Maybe he'll have settled down by tomorrow. Doris Harris wanted to come with us, but he ranted on at her when you were upstairs getting your dog about wasting good money on fish and chips when she had already eaten.'

There was a scream of delight from the Brett children. Heather had placed the three-year-old Fiona on Towser's back. Towser was standing patiently, looking puzzled, his eyes rolling in Hamish's direction for help.

'Leave him be,' shouted Hamish. Heather obediently lifted Fiona off Towser's back and Towser lolloped up the beach and lay panting at Hamish's feet.

'Time I got those kids in bed,' said June. 'They've been on the train all day.'

'Come far?' asked Hamish.

'From London.'

Dermott got to his feet and brushed sand from his trousers. He walked up to the children and swung the toddler on to his shoulders. June joined him, and the family set off together in the direction of the boarding-house.

'That's a nice family,' said Miss Gunnery, returning from a rubbish bin on the other side of the shingle, where she had put the papers. 'Perhaps we should be getting back as well.'

'Whit aboot the night-life o' Skag?' sniggered Cheryl. 'Me and Tracey'd like a drink.'

'How old are you?' demanded Miss Gunnery severely.

Cheryl tossed her long blonde hair. 'Old enough,' she said. Her heavily made-up eyes flirted at Hamish. 'Aye, old enough fur anything, isn't that right, Tracey?'

'Sure is,' said Tracey in a dreadful imitation American accent. 'So let's just mosey along to the pub.'

'Bound to be bottled beer up here,' said Andrew, 'but I'm willing to try it. What about you, Hamish?'

'As long as they'll let Towser in.'

'He's married tae his dug!' shrieked Cheryl.

Hamish's thin, sensitive face flushed angrily. He was ashamed of his affection for his dog, ashamed sometimes of Towser's yellowish mongrel appearance.

'I think a drink's just what we all need,' said Andrew quickly. 'Come along, Hamish.'

Hamish had a sudden desire to sulk. But Miss Gunnery said, 'I saw the pub near the harbour. It looked quite pretty. I think I'll go after all.' She linked a bony arm in Hamish's as he stood up and the small party set off.

It was a pretty thatched pub with tubs of flowers at the door, more like an English inn than a Scottish one. But inside it was as plastic and dreary as the worst of Scottish pubs. A jukebox blared in the corner and a spotty moron was operating the fruit machine with monotonous regularity, his mouth hanging open as he fed in the coins. Hamish had noticed a table and chairs outside and suggested they take their drinks there: Cheryl and Tracey had rums and Coke, Miss Gunnery, a gin and tonic, Andrew, a bottle of beer, and Hamish, a whisky and a bag of potato crisps for Towser.

'There's a carnival here tomorrow,' said Hamish. 'Sideshows and everything. I saw a poster about it on the pub wall.'

'I didn't see a fairground,' said Andrew.

'It'll be here tomorrow all right,' said Hamish, wise in the ways of Highland gypsies. 'They come in the night like a medieval army and the next day, there they all are.'

They finished their drinks and walked slowly back to the boarding-house. Cheryl and Tracey had decided to compete for the attention of Hamish Macbeth and so they walked arm in arm with him while Miss Gunnery and Andrew followed behind.

When they went into the boarding-house, Hamish collected a couple of paperbacks from the bookshelves in the lounge and went up the stairs to his room.

It was then that he found out that the Harrises had the room next door. Bob Harris's voice rose and fell, going on and on and on, punctuated by an occasional whimper from his wife.

Hamish wondered whether to go next door and tell the man to shut up, but as a policeman he had found out the folly of interfering in marital problems. Doris would probably round on him and tell him to leave her husband alone.

Or rather, that's what the lazy Hamish Macbeth told himself.

Chapter Two

A tart temper never mellows with age, and a sharp tongue is the only edged tool that grows keener with constant use.

– Washington Irving

Hamish rose early and took Towser for a walk along the deserted dunes outside the hotel. The day was grey and warm and misty. Somewhere a foghorn sounded like some lost sea creature. The midges, those pestilent Scottish mosquitoes which he had naïvely thought he had left behind him on the west coast, were out in force. He automatically felt in his shirt pocket for a stick of repellent and found he had none and remembered there was one in his suitcase.

He returned to his room and pulled his suitcase out from under the bed and flipped back the lid. It was then that he realized it had been searched. It was not precisely that things had been disturbed; there was more a *smell*, a feeling, that things had been gone through. Not that there was much left in the suitcase. He had unpacked nearly everything. He found a stick of repellent in one of the pockets lining the back of the case. There were a few books and sweaters he had not yet put away in the drawers, and oh, God, his police identification card, his notebook, and a pair of handcuffs. He sat back on his heels, his mind ranging busily over the guests. He had not bothered to lock his bedroom door when he had gone out with Towser. Rogers? Was it plain nosiness? He could complain, and complain loudly, but he had no real proof. He fished out the suitcase keys from a back pocket and locked the case and pushed it back under the bed. Pointless thing to bother about doing now. Someone in this hotel now knew he was a policeman. He would study their reactions to him today.

The only good thing about breakfast was the surly silence of Bob Harris. The food was awful: fried haggis and watery eggs; hard, dry rolls with margarine; and marmalade so thin it could have been watered.

'I'm going to the carnival,' said Hamish to Miss Gunnery. 'Would you like to come?'

Before she could reply, Dermott Brett called over. 'Going to the carnival? We'll come too, Hamish, and take the kids.'

And so, to Miss Gunnery's disappointment, for she had murmured to Hamish, 'I hate crowds,' the others came along as well, minus the Harrises. They had gone a little way towards Skag when the sound of running footsteps made them turn around. Doris Harris was running to catch up with them, her face flushed.

'Bob doesn't want to come,' she said breathlessly.

As they walked on, they all found they were searching for new topics of conversation, the main one having hitherto been what a pig Bob Harris was. Hamish's stick of repellent was gradually getting worn down as everyone kept borrowing it. Hands flapped at the stinging, biting midges. 'Let's hope they leave us when we get to the carnival,' said Hamish. A thin drizzle had started to fall.

An air of gloom was descending on the party. Hamish had a desire to lighten it for Doris's sake. Her life with Bob was surely misery enough. She should enjoy this bit of freedom. He stared up at the sky, willing the weather to change. There was a whisper of a breeze against his cheek. 'Anyone heard the weather forecast?' he asked.

'Said it might get sunny later,' said Andrew.

The children began to chatter with excitement, for the fair was now in view in a field outside Skag.

Hamish looked at his watch. 'There're floats and some sort of procession through the village first. Let's go and watch that.'

The rain was falling heavier as they huddled in a group and watched a series of tacky floats move past. A Scottish bank had a traditional jazz band on the back of a truck which momentarily brightened things as it slowly cruised by them, but the rest of the floats were mostly tableaux by the children, wet children with grease-paint running down their faces in the rain. Then there was the crowning of the carnival queen, a singularly ill-favoured little girl; but as Hamish learned, she was the daughter of the publican, who had contributed a large sum of money to the carnival, so that explained the choice.

They all walked with Hamish to the fair-ground, all occasionally looking hopefully at him like tourists at their guide.

'I know,' said Hamish, 'let's go on the dodgem cars. What about it, Miss Gunnery?'

'It's a mither complex, that's whit it is,' said Cheryl sourly to Tracey, but Hamish decided to ignore the gibe. And then, as they crashed their way about in the dodgem cars, Doris with Andrew, Hamish with Miss Gunnery, Cheryl and Tracey screaming together and eyeing the local talent, Dermott and June with their toddler on their knee while the other two children took up another car, the weather made one of its lightning changes. Again the grey rolled back out to sea, like a curtain being swept back on the transformation scene in a pantomime.

After the dodgems, Hamish bought candy floss for the children and then looked about for more amusement. He was determined to keep 'his' little party happy. He was beginning to catch a glimpse of his own easygoing happiness coming back again and he did not want to lose it. So they obediently followed him to the ghost train and he had the delight and pleasure of hearing the prim Miss Gunnery beside him in the car shrieking her head off. She gave him a rueful look afterwards. 'I don't often let my hair down like that.'

Hamish looked at her glossy brown hair, which was scraped into a severe knot on top of her head. 'You should,' he said. 'You've got pretty hair.'

Miss Gunnery gave him such a warm glowing look that he moved away from her uneasily. But he found that leaving her side was to get the undivided attention of Cheryl and Tracey, so he returned to her and continued to lead his party on and off roundabouts all over the fairground until Dermott Brett said the children were weary and it was nearly time for tea. They had made a lunch of hot dogs, candy floss and chocolate bars, and as they all headed back to the hotel, the thought of the tea that was probably awaiting them dampened their appetites further.

The Brett children began to invent awful menus from fried snails to roast baby until they were helpless with giggles. Doris was laughing. She looked a changed woman. Hamish thought she had probably been quite pretty when she was younger. Andrew Biggar was walking beside her, looking delighted with her company.

Hamish, covertly watching them, began to feel uneasy. He felt he was looking at the ingredients for a disaster: crushed wife, nasty husband, gentle and decent man – mix all together and what do you get? Murder, said a voice in his brain.

He shook himself to get rid of the thought. Husbands and wives nagged each other up and down the length of the British Isles, but they didn't murder each other – or not all of them did.

The main dish of high tea was a mixed grill: one small sausage, one kidney, one tomato and the inevitable chips. Bob Harris was there, and drunk. He was so drunk that his voice was lowered to an almost incomprehensible whining mumble. Hamish was just able to make out that the burden of his complaint was that Doris had actually defied him by going off to the fair.

After tea, Doris got to her feet and said quietly that she was tired and was going to have an early night. They all expected Bob

Harris to join her but he followed them through to the lounge, just sober enough after the dreadful tea to turn his viciousness on the group. His first target was Andrew Biggar. 'You army men are all the same,' he jeered. 'The only reason you go into the army is because you can't adapt to civilian life. Have to be told what to do.'

Andrew, who had picked up a book, put it down and said evenly, 'Just shut up.'

Heather, the seven-year-old, gave a nervous laugh. Bob's bulbous eyes focused on the child. 'Your trouble is, you're spoilt,' he said.

'Here, that's enough,' protested Dermott. 'Why don't you go upstairs and sleep it off.'

'I can hold my drink,' said Bob truculently. 'And don't you come the high and mighty with me. I could tell this lot a thing or two about you and –'

'I'm taking the children up to bed and out of this,' shouted June. She gathered up the toddler and left, with the other two children following close behind.

'You are one of the nastiest men I have ever come across,' said Miss Gunnery.

'Well, there can't be many men who've come across you, or got their leg over you, if any,' sneered Bob. 'You remind me of an old dried-up stick of a French teacher I used to have. You –'

He let out a yelp of pain. Hamish Macbeth had twisted his arm up his back. 'Off to bed,' said Hamish pleasantly. He marched him to the door, released him and shoved him outside and slammed the door in his face.

'That's that,' said Hamish as Dermott, Andrew and Miss Gunnery, Cheryl and Tracey stared at him in awe. He looked out of the window. 'The sun's still blazing down. Anyone brave enough for a swim?'

'I think I would like that,' said Miss Gunnery, surprising them all.

'Wait till you see what we've got to wear,' cried Cheryl.

Andrew said quietly, 'I wonder if Doris would like to come.'

'I wouldn't bother,' said Hamish quickly.

But when they all had gathered in the hall, that is Miss Gunnery, Hamish, Cheryl and Tracey and Andrew Biggar, Doris came down the stairs to join them, carrying a large beach towel over one arm.

'Bob's asleep,' she said. 'Andrew heard the snores through the door, so he knocked and told me you were going.'

Hamish looked at Andrew and Doris uneasily. They made such a suitable couple. He fought down a nagging feeling of apprehension.

The party walked across the sand dunes in front of the hotel and then over the shingle rise which ran all the way from the harbour along the back of the beach and so down to the blowing sand. The sun was very warm for Scotland.

They were all wearing their bathing-costumes under their clothes. Tracey and Cheryl stripped down to string bikinis, exposing skinny acres of shark's-belly-white skin. Miss Gunnery was wearing a modest one-piece. She had a surprisingly trim, muscled, if flat-chested body and long legs. Doris, also in a one-piece, ran down to the water with Andrew, plunged in and then let out a scream. 'It's *freezing*!' she called back.

Hamish, used to swimming in cold Highland streams and lochs, found the waters of the North Sea quite bearable. But the others gave up quite quickly and huddled in their beach towels, and when Hamish came running up the beach, they turned to him like hopeful children.

'There's still the fair,' he said, 'unless you're all tired of it.'

This was hailed with enthusiasm, so they went back to the boarding-house to change. Doris was carrying a beach bag, and with a little guilty flush, she asked Miss Gunnery if she could use her room to change, '. . . so as not to disturb Bob.'

Hamish again felt that uneasiness as Miss Gunnery agreed. He felt they were all becoming conspirators in encouraging a highly dangerous romance between Doris and Andrew Biggar.

The Bretts were seated in the lounge. They looked wistful when they heard the others were going to the fair, but they had better stay and look after the children.

Hamish found himself cursing Bob Harris again as they all set out. Normally, they would have remained a typical group of British holiday-makers, restrained and separate and wary of each other. But the common resentment against the nag had drawn them all together so quickly, which might have been a good thing had it not been for the shy glow on Doris's face when she looked at Andrew.

He had a sudden sharp longing for Priscilla Halburton-Smythe's cool assessment of the situation. But Priscilla, his ex-fiancée, was down in England. She had seemed very comfortable and at ease in his company before she had left. Whatever she had once felt for him – and he often wondered now what that something had been – had gone. And what am I doing, Hamish Macbeth, he wondered, holidaying with this odd bunch? He automatically stooped to pat Towser for comfort and then remembered he had left the dog behind at the boarding-house.

As they approached Skag, the wind rose, making the sands sing, blowing white sand about them so that they were glad to get in amongst the comparative shelter of the fair booths and roundabouts. Hamish waited until they all had piled on to a roundabout and then slid off quietly to see a bit of Skag and have some time to himself. He wandered away from the fairground, hearing the harsh carousel music fading behind him, reaching him only now and then in snatches borne by the ever-increasing wind. He walked through the narrow streets, noticing, here and there, the larger window in front of a cottage denoting that it was once a shop, before the days of cars and cheap supermarkets at the nearest town. Some of the cottages were thatched, odd in Scotland, when the only cottages that were once thatched had been the black houses covered in heather, the ones without chimneys, now only maintained as museum pieces. And yet the buildings were surely not that old, late Victorian, perhaps. He saw a building with a sign 'Museum' outside and went in for a look around.

There had evidently been a village on the point between the river Skag and the North Sea for as long as anyone could remember, but in the 1880s, weeks of torrential rain and high winds and high tides had caused river and sea to meet in one roaring flood which had covered the whole village. The village had remained drowned for weeks before the waters had receded. Ten years later, when the village had been rebuilt and was thriving again, great gales had come tearing over the North Sea from Scandinavia, whipping up the white sand and eventually burying the whole village. After the houses had been excavated, trees and razor-grass had been planted on the other side of the river, where a Scottish Sahara of white sand dunes stretched for miles to stop the sand from shifting.

He bought a small book on the history of the village and went back out without stopping to look at any of the exhibits in glass cases. The narrow, unsurfaced streets were deserted. Ribbons of sand snaked along them like feelers put out by some alien creature. The trouble with Scottish villages like this, thought Hamish, was that all the community life had been bled out of them. Cars took the villagers out at night to the bright lights of the town. The villagers would often blame the incomers for having destroyed village life, but it was the automobile which had done that, making nomads of even the elderly. There was no putting the clock back now.

And then Hamish thought he was falling into the messy ways of thinking of so many – that the good old days had been better. Not so long ago, Skag would have been a closed-in fishing community, repressed and dark and secretive, everything kept under wraps – incest, drunkenness, violence, child abuse, pregnant girls forced to marry men who did not want them, all the miseries coloured by the overriding horror of living in poverty or the fear of having to.

So now the young people left the quiet Scottish villages and were replaced by incomers from the south, who claimed they had come in search of 'the quality of life' which meant they got regularly drunk with all the other incomers fleeing from reality. But the village did have an odd eerie charm, filled as it was with the sound of rushing water from the river and the susurration of the gritty white sand blowing in the streets. There was one shop still open, manned by the inevitable Asian. A Scottish shopkeeper closed up at teatime, no matter how bad trade was. It sold newspapers, sweets, postcards and toys, and an odd assortment of household goods. Next to it was a dress-shop, Paris Fashions, with two dresses drooping in the window and with price-tags marking the gowns down from £120 to £85. Hamish wondered if they would ever sell. But where teashops used to be the last refuge of the genteel, now it was dress-shops, which opened their doors for a few months before facing up to the fact that with cheap clothes so near at hand in the local town, it was folly to try to sell Bond Street fashions at Bond Street prices.

There were two churches, one Free Church of Scotland and one Church of Scotland. A poster outside the Church of Scotland was half torn and fluttering in the wind. It said, 'Life is Fragile. Handle with Prayer.'

Turning away from it, Hamish saw Bob Harris. He was coming out of a house at the end of the main street, his walk denoting that he was still drunk. His face was flushed and he had a triumphant smile on his face. He's just made someone's life a misery, thought Hamish. I wonder who lives there. Then he suddenly did not want to know anything more about Bob Harris and about whom he had been possibly persecuting. He walked instead to the harbour and sat on a bollard and looked down into the water.

The wind suddenly dropped and all was very quiet and still. He reflected that it must be the turn of the tide. It was a phenomenon he had noticed before. Just at the turn of the tide, nature held its breath – no bird sang, everything seemed to be waiting and waiting. And then, sure enough, as if someone had flicked a switch, everything started in motion again.

He got up and decided to go straight back to the hotel, collect a couple of paperbacks, and walk Towser along the beach. He occasionally wondered who it was who had searched his case but decided it had probably been Rogers, whose motive had been nothing more sinister than vulgar curiosity.

He felt a pang of guilt at not rejoining the others, but then reminded himself severely that he was not related to them, barely knew them, neither was he on police duty. If Bob Harris murdered his wife, then that was his business. And so, comforting himself with these callous thoughts, he loped home, collected Towser and the paperbacks, and set out along the beach in the opposite direction from Skag. He found a comfortable hollow and settled down to read with Towser at his feet. It would not get really dark. A pearly twilight would settle down about one in the morning for about two hours.

He read a tough-cop American detective story. The detective in it seemed to get results by punching confessions out of people, which gave Hamish a vicarious thrill as he thought of the scandal and miles of red tape that would descend on his head if he tried to do the same thing. The story ended satisfactorily with the detective incinerating the villains in a warehouse and getting a medal for bravery from the mayor in front of a cheering crowd on the steps of City Hall. America must be a marvellous country, thought Hamish wryly, if any of this was real. He imagined what would happen to him if he did the same thing. He would be hauled up before his superiors, who would want to know first of all why he had tackled the villians single-handed and not called for back-up, and why he had wrecked three police cars. Then he would be told that when he had finished writing all that out in triplicate, he would be interviewed by the gentlemen who owned the warehouse and their insurance company to explain why he had torched billions of dollars' worth of stock.

With a sigh of satisfaction, he stood up and stretched and set off back along the beach for the boarding-house.

He had been looking forward to reading the other book, but Bob Harris was berating his wife next door and she was crying. Hamish ripped up pieces of tissue paper to form earplugs, buried his head under the pillow and fell asleep.

Hamish had fully intended to keep the next day for himself, but when he entered the dining room for breakfast, all eyes turned to him hopefully. It was the sight of Doris's sad face that made up his mind for him. He suddenly did not care whether Doris fell in love with Andrew or not. She might have a little happiness to remember in her otherwise miserable life.

'Whit are we daein' the day, Hamish?' Cheryl called over to him.

'I thought you would all have had enough of bloody civil servants,' growled Bob Harris. 'Petty little bureaucrats.'

Hamish ignored him. 'I was down at the harbour yesterday evening,' he said, 'and I noticed that you can hire a boat and fishing tackle. Anyone for fishing?'

They all agreed, with the exception of Bob, who sneered, 'Fishing's for fools.'

Dermott Brett said he would take his car into Skag because he didn't want the children too tired with the walk before the day started. 'Are you taking Towser?' asked Heather.

'Yes,' said Hamish. 'He likes boats.'

Miss Gunnery said she would take her car as well and offered Hamish a lift. She frowned when Cheryl and Tracey begged a lift as well but said reluctantly that they could come too. Andrew and Doris said nothing. Hamish sensed a *waiting* in Doris. She was hoping she could slip away.

Nonetheless he was surprised when they all gathered on the harbour to find that Andrew had driven Doris in his car.

'Where's Bob?' asked Dermott.

'He doesn't want to come,' said Doris curtly.

They went to a hut at the back of the harbour where a surly man said he would supply them with tackle and take them out. They all paid their share of the cost. It was a large open boat with an outboard. The day was grey and still, the water flat and oily.

The boat owner, Jamie MacPherson, issued them with old lifejackets and even found some small ones for the children. He tried to object to Towser until he saw the party was going to cancel the trip if the dog wasn't allowed on board.

They all climbed down a seaweed-slippery ladder from the jetty and on to the boat. Hamish had taken a dislike to Jamie, but he had to admit the man was efficient. He had small rods for Heather and Callum and even a small stick with a thread and a bent pin on it for the toddler, Fiona. They chugged out into the North Sea until the boat stopped and they began to rig up their lines. There were various false alarms. Doris caught a bit of seaweed and June Brett, an old shoe.

The day was hazy and lazy and then Heather said suddenly, 'Someone ought to kill Mr Harris.'

'That's enough of that, miss,' said her mother sharply and then looked apologetically at Doris.

'A lot of people want to kill Bob,' said Doris. 'Don't get angry with the child.'

'Why did you marry him?' asked Heather in her clear piping voice.

'People change,' said Doris on a sigh.

'It's not easy to kill someone,' said Hamish, wondering if one of them might betray that he or she had searched his suitcase and knew he was a policeman.

Andrew laughed and then asked the question Hamish had been dreading. 'Which branch of the civil service are you in, Hamish?'

'Min of Ag and Fish,' said Hamish, meaning the Ministry of Agriculture and Fisheries.

'Anyone there you would like to kill?'

'Aye,' said Hamish, thinking of the bane of his life, Detective Chief Inspector Blair, 'there's this big fat Glaswegian wi' a sewer mouth.'

'I always think the best murders are when they are committed by someone who doesn't know the victim,' said Miss Gunnery.

'There iss no such thing as a good murder,' said Hamish repressively. His Highland accent took on that sibilancy it always did when he was upset. 'There iss nothing good in the taking of another's life.'

'Well, I think that awfy Bob Harris waud be better dead,' said Tracey.

'Please do not say such things in front of Doris,' said Andrew sharply.

'She waud be glad tae see the last o' him,' retorted Cheryl.

'In a book I was reading at school, the wicked girl in the remove was killed with a rare South African poison,' said Heather.

'You won't get rare South African poisons in Skag,' said Hamish. 'Murders are usually done in rage and they're dreary and simple – a blow tae the head, a push down the stairs, an electric heater chucked in the bath, or something that looks like a climbing accident.'

'If he had come with us,' said Heather eagerly, 'we could have pushed him overboard and said it was an accident.'

'What about Mr MacPherson there?' said Hamish, jerking his thumb at the surly man at the tiller.

'We would need to pay him hush money,' said Heather.

She was told sharply by her mother to be quiet, but the fish weren't biting and somehow the subject of killing Bob Harris just wouldn't go away. Miss Gunnery raised a laugh by saying the food at the boarding-house was enough to kill anyone, and that started a discussion of the various methods of poisoning, from simple broken glass in the pudding to arsenic in the tea.

Hamish was relieved when they drifted into a shoal of mackerel and shrieks of excitement as the fish were landed drove thoughts of murder out of the heads of the party. Hamish agreed as they made their way back to the harbour that he would phone the hotel and tell the Rogerses that he would cook the mackerel for their tea. They ate sandwiches in the pub and then headed home with their catch, Hamish having found out that there was to be a dance in the Church of Scotland hall that evening and suggesting they all go. Dermott said he would stay behind with the children so that June could have a night out. They seemed to have the ideal marriage.

He did not expect that Doris would be able to go with them, but Bob Harris was absent from the tea table as they laughed and joked and ate grilled mackerel and voted Hamish cook of the year.

They gathered in the lounge to sort out who would go in which car. Cheryl and Tracey were both wearing very short black leather skirts with very high heels and skimpy tops with plunging necklines. Their blonded hair had been backcombed and left to stand on end. Miss Gunnery was a surprise. She had left off her glasses and her brown hair was combed down to her shoulders, soft and wavy. She was wearing a plain white blouse and black skirt and modest heels but she looked softer and more vulnerable. June was amazing in a shocking-pink chiffon dress with thin straps and a fake diamond necklace. Doris Brett had brushed down her hair and put on a plain black dress. She had a very good figure and Hamish noticed gloomily that Andrew Biggar was taking in that fact as well.

Miss Gunnery asked Hamish to drive her car, saying she couldn't see a thing without her glasses. Cheryl and Tracey went with them.

Hamish had thought it would be a sort of ceilidh with reels and country dances, but it turned out to be a disco full of thin, badly nourished teenagers, brought up on a diet of bread and frozen food. Scotland has one of the worst diets in the world, shunning fresh fruit and green vegetables. Scotland is also famous for bad teeth and Hamish noticed that some of the young teenagers had dentures. The old idea still prevailed. If you have a toothache, get the tooth extracted.

'I can't do that sort of dancing,' said Miss Gunnery. 'They look like a lot of dervishes.'

'Oh, you jist throw yourself around,' said Hamish amiably. 'Follow me.'

His long, gangling figure threw itself this way and that, and since his movements seemed to have absolutely nothing to do with the beat of the music, the others joined him on the floor. If Hamish could make such a fool of himself, then they could, too.

It turned out to be a happy evening, and the teenagers who came up to talk to them turned into ordinary pleasant young people. One youth approached Hamish and whispered, 'Hey, Mac, we got a drink outside.' Glad to see some of the old Highland traditions still existed, Hamish followed him outside, where he joined a group of youths. One passed him a half bottle of Scotch and Hamish took a hearty swig.

'Nice to see young people still around the villages,' he said. 'I thought you would all be in town for the evening.'

'We hiv our ain fun,' said one, proving it by lighting up a joint. 'Fancy a bit o' skirt, grand-dad?'

Hamish, who was in his thirties, ignored the 'grand-dad' and the smell of cannabis. He was on holiday, and unless someone slew someone in front of him, he did not plan to become a policeman again until the holiday was over.

'I'm with my own party,' he said amiably.

'Och, them,' said the youth derisively. 'I mean bint, get a leg ower.'

'Oh,' said Hamish, the light dawning. 'You mean a brothel.'

'Aye, Maggie Simpson's, down the end of the main street.'

Hamish wondered suddenly if that had been the house he had seen Bob Harris leaving. 'Not tonight,' he said. He crossed the road to the pub, bought a half bottle of whisky, and returned and passed it around. He found that not one of the youths was employed, that all dreamt of going to London or Glasgow. The boredom of their days was alleviated by a combination of drink, hash and videos. And yet they seemed a nice enough bunch. A generation or two ago, before the dole was enough to drink on, they would have found work in fishing or farming. But they were as much slaves to pleasure and idleness as any dilettante aristocrat of a century ago.

He went back into the church hall and stared in delight at the spectacle of Miss Gunnery dancing with a slim leatherclad youth. Miss Gunnery appeared to have left her inhibitions behind with her glasses and hairpins. She was shaking and moving with the best of them. In a dark corner of the hall, Doris and Andrew were sitting side by side, talking intensely.

He took June Brett up for a dance, but she said she couldn't abide 'this modern stuff' and insisted on shuffling around trying to get him to do a foxtrot to a disco beat.

Hamish could not but help feeling pleased with himself. He knew his efforts were making it a happy holiday, even for such as the dreadful Cheryl and Tracey, who were dancing with stiff stork-like movements in their very high heels, their faces animated under their masks of dead-white make-up and purple eye-shadow.

It certainly never crossed his mind that this would be their last happy evening together, and that he himself would do something before the night was out that would start a chain of events leading to murder.

Chapter Three

Fighting is all a mistake, friend Eric,
And has been so since the age Homeric . . .
–Adam Lindsay Gordon

When they arrived back at the boarding-house, Hamish noticed the way Doris's anxious eyes flew to an upstairs window. A light was shining out into the odd twilight which replaces darkness in a northern summer. That would be her room, thought Hamish, the one at the front, next to mine.

Inside, he said his goodnights and made his way upstairs and then took Towser out along the beach for a walk. As soon as he returned to his room, he heard Bob Harris's voice, loud and clear. 'What the hell do you think you were doing, dressing up like a tart? Get that muck off your face. You look like a whore. A dance in a church? Are you out of your head? I don't know why I put up with you. You make me sick. You go around making sheep's eyes at men, but no one notices you. You're insignificant. Always were. God knows why I married you.'

Doris whimpered something and then began to cry.

The nag's voice went on. 'Of course, you think that Biggar chap is interested in you but he's just playing the gallant officer and gentleman. Never been married, I should guess. Too much fun with the chaps, if you ask me.'

Then Doris's voice, shrill and defiant, 'He's *not* gay! You're *horrible.*'

There was the sound of a smack, followed by a wail of pain from Doris.

Without stopping to think, Hamish went next door and hammered on it. Bob Harris opened the door, his face flushed with drink.

'What do you want?' he snarled.

Hamish shouted, 'Look, man, I'm trying to have a peaceful night, and if you don't stop nagging your wife, I'll kill you, you bastard!'

The normally mild-mannered Hamish heard the echoes of his voice echoing around the silent house, the *listening* house.

'You long drip of nothing!' Bob Harris swung a punch at Hamish, who blocked it and then socked him right in the nose.

'Jist shut up!' roared Hamish.

He went back to his room and slammed the door.

An almost eerie silence fell on the boarding-house. Hamish shrugged. He hoped that would shut the nag up for the rest of the holiday.

The residents of The Friendly House awoke to a new day. Mr Rogers, enjoying the first cup of coffee of the day, said to his wife, 'Did you hear that rumpus last night?'

'Aye,' said Mrs Rogers. 'I heard that Macbeth fellow threatening to kill Harris.'

'Someone *should* kill him.' Mr Rogers moodily stirred his coffee, a new brand, miles cheaper than anything else on the market and tasting as if it were made from dandelion roots instead of coffee beans. 'D'ye know what he said to me last night, afore his wife came back wi' the others?'

Mrs Rogers was silent. She had heard all about what Bob Harris had said to her husband, but to point this out would just make him furious. Like most men with a bad memory, Mr Rogers considered that everyone else in general and his wife in particular were the ones with bad memories.

'He says to me, he says, "I am going to report your place to the tourist board as a cheap-skate outfit. The food's vile." Can you credit that? Cheek! The place is the cheapest in

Scotland for the price. Whit does he expect, champagne and caviare?'

'Can't stop him,' said Mrs Rogers.

Mr Rogers stirred his coffee ferociously. 'Ho, no? We'll see about that.'

'Was that our Hamish on the war-path?' June asked Dermott as she dressed Fiona.

'He was saying as how he would kill Bob and then I think he socked him one.'

'I can't see Hamish hitting anyone. Probably that bastard was punching Doris at the time.'

'Hamish said he would kill him.'

'Not a bad idea. You know what Bob's threatening to do?'

Dermott walked to the window and looked out. His fat face was creased with worry. 'He wouldn't actually do it, June. Would he?'

'I don't know. How will we stop him?'

'Maybe Hamish will kill him,' said Dermott with a harsh laugh. 'That would solve all our problems.'

Miss Gunnery, Andrew, Cheryl and Tracey were the first in the breakfast room. Cheryl's eyes gleamed with excitement. 'Well, whit did ye think o' last night?'

'I enjoyed the dance,' said Miss Gunnery, primly shaking out her paper napkin and noticing with a frown that it was the same one she had had since she arrived. Surely the Rogerses did not expect one paper napkin each to last the whole stay?

'Wisnae talking about the dance, wis we, Tracey?' said Cheryl. 'Its aboot Hamish. Did ye hear the row?'

'I never listen to other people's conversations,' said Miss Gunnery repressively.

'Ye couldnae miss hearing it,' pointed out Tracey. 'First it was Bob giving Doris laldy, saying as how Andrew was a poofter. Then Hamish tells him to shut it and next thing I hears is Hamish saying he'll kill him and the sound of a blow.'

'I am amazed such as Bob Harris has managed to live this long,' said Miss Gunnery. 'Mr Macbeth is a gentleman and no doubt the provocation was great. Do you not think so, Mr Biggar?'

Andrew looked up from the book he was reading. 'The man bores me,' he said shortly. 'But, yes, he ought to be put down.'

They fell silent as Bob Harris came in on his own. Cheryl and Tracey stared avidly at his swollen nose. Then Hamish entered, said a cheerful, 'Good morning' all round and took his place at the table.

He was just about to strike up a conversation with Miss Gunnery, mainly to ignore the glowering looks he was getting from Bob, when two policemen entered the dining room, and behind them came Doris, who slipped quietly into her chair.

'Mr Harris?' asked the first policeman, looking around.

'That's me,' said Bob truculently.

'I am Police Constable Paul Crick, and this is Police Constable Peter Emett. You phoned the station this morning?'

'Yes.' Bob Harris got to his feet. 'I want to charge this man, Hamish Macbeth, with assault.'

'Which is Mr Macbeth?'

Hamish stood up as well.

'Well,' said Paul Crick, 'if you two gentlemen will jist step outside.'

'You can use the lounge,' said Mr Rogers.

He ushered the small party across the hall.

'Tell us what happened,' said Crick after he had closed the door of the lounge on Mr Rogers. 'We'll begin at the beginning. Your name is Mr Robert Harris, is it not?'

'Yes.'

'Your address?'

'Elmlea, South Bewdley Road, Evesham.'

'Aye, that would be in Worcestershire.'

'Correct.'

'Job?'

'Double-glazing salesman.'

Crick turned to Hamish. Hamish knew he would need to tell them he was a policeman.

They would probably haul him off down to the station. The very idea that one of their own had been involved in any misdemeanor was enough to make them more harsh than they would be towards an ordinary member of the public.

The door opened and Doris and Miss Gunnery stood there. 'You must not listen to my husband,' said Doris. 'Hamish was protecting himself. My husband attacked him.'

'You bitch!' roared Bob Harris.

'I heard the whole thing, as did the other residents,' declared Miss Gunnery. 'Mr Harris had been keeping us awake by shouting at his wife.'

Crick looked at Hamish. 'Is this true?'

'He tried to punch me,' said Hamish. 'Yes, I was defending myself.' He knew this to be true. He had felt a great wave of satisfaction when his own punch had connected with Bob's nose.

Crick flicked his notebook closed and turned to Bob. 'Before you go ahead with this complaint, sir,' he said, 'you're not going to get very far wi' it if your ain wife is going to get up in the sheriff's court and say it was your fault.'

'And the rest of us,' said Miss Gunnery.

'The hell with the lot of you,' roared Bob Harris. 'You Scotch police are so damn lazy, you just don't want to investigate anything.'

'You'd better watch your mouth,' snapped Crick. 'Do you want to proceed with this charge or not?'

'Forget it, forget it.' Bob pushed his way roughly past his wife and Miss Gunnery and left the room.

Crick and Emett turned to Hamish. They were remarkably alike, being quite small for policemen, and both with sandy hair and pale-grey eyes. 'Don't be so handy wi' your fists in future, Mr Macbeth,' said Crick.

They both left. 'That was verra good of you,' said Hamish to Doris, 'but he'll never forgive you.'

'Never forgive me, never forgive me,' said Doris tearfully. 'Well, he can add it to the mile-long list of things he's never going to forgive me for . . . breathing being one of them.'

She buried her face in Miss Gunnery's thin shoulder and began to sob.

Hamish walked out quickly. He was weary of the people in the boarding-house and homesick for Lochdubh. He did not return to the breakfast room but collected Towser and headed along the beach, moodily throwing stones into the sea.

At last he returned. He saw, as he approached, the small figure of Doris Harris hurrying off in the direction of the village. When he went in, the boarding-house was silent. Not a sound. He settled Towser in the bedroom with a bowl of food and a bowl of fresh water and went out again, this time towards Skag, but keeping a wary eye out for any of the other residents so that he could avoid them.

Outside a musty shop that sold second-hand goods of the kind that no antique dealer would want was a wooden stand filled with paperbacks. He selected a couple and walked out of the village to a grassy bank at a bend of the river, sat with his back against the sun-warmed wall of a shed and began to read to fight down a feeling of dread. There was every reason to be afraid that something nasty was going to happen at that boarding-house containing such combustible material. The day was sunny and pleasant and he concentrated on his reading to such good effect that he had finished two books by tea-time. Reluctant to return to the boarding-house for another nasty high tea, he went to the fish-and-chips shop and, armed with a paper packet of fish and chips, he walked to the harbour jetty and ate placidly, relaxed now, beginning to think about his dog and realizing he should really return and give Towser a walk.

He crumpled up his fish-supper paper and threw it in a rubbish bin and strolled to the edge of the jetty and looked down into the receding waters. The harbour jetty thrust out into the river Skag just below a point where it flowed into the North Sea. The tide was ebbing fast. At low tide, the foot of the jetty was left dry, with the river running between sandbanks to the sea.

He stared idly down into the receding water. It was a lovely, calm late afternoon, with a sky like pearl. Children's voices sounded on the still air and seagulls cruised lazily overhead.

Bob Harris came suddenly back into Hamish's mind and he felt all his old dread returning.

And then, as he looked over the edge of the jetty, a distorted face stared back up at Hamish. He had been thinking about Bob Harris, cursing Bob Harris, so that at first he thought that the dreadful man had stamped his image on his mind. Then, as the water sank lower, he saw lank hair rising and falling like seaweed, he saw the way pale bulbous eyes stared up at him with an expression of outrage.

He climbed down the ladder attached to the wooden jetty and dragged the body clear of the water. Although he desperately tried every means of artificial respiration, he knew as he worked that it was hopeless. Bob Harris was very dead and had probably been dead for some hours.

A man peered over the jetty and shouted to him. Hamish told him to fetch the police.

Hamish turned the body gently over and parted the damp hair. Someone had struck Bob a savage blow on the back of the head. He sat down on the wet sand and stared bleakly out at the receding water. There was surely no hope that Bob had got drunk and fallen into the water. This was murder. But still, he thought suddenly, he *could* be wrong. Perhaps Bob *had* fallen over and struck his head on something. But there were no rocks and no sign of blood on the piers of the jetty. Of course, it depended on the time he had fallen in. If the tide was high and he had struck his head on some part of the jetty structure, then any blood and hair would have been washed away.

He heard the approaching wail of a police siren. There would be no hope now of concealing his profession.

Soon he was surrounded by policemen and then forensic men and then arrived Detective Inspector Sandy Deacon, a small, ferrety man with suspicious eyes. Hamish patiently answered questions about the finding of the body, of what he knew about Bob Harris, which was very little. Yes, he was the man who had punched Harris in self-defence.

'Odd behaviour for a police constable,' said Deacon sourly. Hamish requested that he be allowed to return to the boarding-house, as his dog needed a walk.

'No, you don't, laddie,' said Deacon. 'Policeman or not, you're our prime suspect!'

Deacon, who came from the nearest town, Dungarton, had found out after one phone call to Superintendent Daviot that Hamish Macbeth had recently been demoted from sergeant, had also recently broken off his engagement to a fine and beautiful lady, and was rather weird.

So Hamish sat and fretted. An office in the village police station had been turned over to the murder inquiry as his 'prison'. He had to sit there, patiently answering questions fired at him by Deacon and a detective sergeant called Johnny Clay. He repeated over and over again that he had spent a solitary day, and no, he did not have any witnesses.

It transpired from a pathologist's preliminary report that Bob Harris had been struck on the head, possibly with a piece of driftwood, for scraps of sea-washed wood had been found embedded in the wound in his scalp. He had been last seen by the boatman who had hired the fishing tackle to the boarding-house party. Bob Harris had been standing on the edge of the jetty, looking out over the water. Before that, he had been seen drinking heavily in the local pub. The boatman, Jamie MacPherson, had also provided the police with the interesting news that all the residents of The Friendly House had been plotting Bob's murder.

Hamish tried to keep his temper. It was an odd and frustrating feeling to experience what it was like to be on the wrong side of the law. He was also worried about Towser, locked up in the boarding-house bedroom. Towser, for all his mongrel faults, was a clean animal and must be suffering agonies rather than foul the room.

Hamish had given up smoking some time ago but now he passionately longed for a cigarette. He was just beginning to think that they meant to keep him in the police station all night when Crick put his head round the door and summoned Deacon from the room.

Deacon switched off the tape recorder and went outside. Clay, the detective sergeant, stared stolidly at Hamish. Then the door opened and Deacon said nastily, 'Get out o' here, Macbeth, and next time ye try to protect a lady's name, don't waste police time doing it!'

Hamish left the interview room, wondering about his remarkable release. At first he did not recognize Miss Gunnery, who was waiting for him with Towser.

She was wearing a smart dress and her hair was down on her shoulders as it had been on the evening of the dance. She was very heavily made up and wearing high heels.

'What happened? What are you doing here?' asked Hamish.

'Oh, do come along, darling,' she said in a simpering voice, quite unlike her usual forthright tones. 'Towser wants his walkies.'

Hamish headed for the front door of the police station but she whispered, 'No, through the back. The press are outside. My car's there.'

A policeman held a door open for them and they went down a short corridor and out into a small yard. 'In the car,' urged Miss Gunnery. 'I'll tell you about it as we drive home.'

She drove out at speed. Flashlights from press cameras nearly blinded her, reporters hammered at the car windows, but soon they were out on the road. 'They're outside the boarding-house as well,' said Miss Gunnery.

'So why was I released so soon?' asked Hamish.

'I knew you didn't do it, and I found out when they questioned me that the murder was supposed to have taken place in the middle of the afternoon, so I . . . don't get mad . . . I told them you had spent the afternoon in bed with me.'

'Oh, my God,' wailed Hamish. 'There wass no need for that, no need at all. They would have gone on giving me a hard time, but then they would haff had to let me go.'

'I thought you would be pleased,' she said in a small voice. 'You . . . you won't tell them I lied?'

'No, I won't do that. But don't effer do such a thing again. How did you get Towser?'

'I borrowed the spare key from Rogers.'

'But the others will know that you weren't with me!'

'No, they were all out somewhere, all of them, even the Rogerses. They all turned up at tea-time to find the police waiting. While I was waiting my turn to be questioned, I got the key and took poor Towser out for a walk.'

'And they let you do it?'

'I didn't ask permission. I returned just when they were questioning Andrew. When it was my turn, I said I would tell them where I had been if they would tell me where you were, for Doris had been interviewed first and told me you had found the body. They said you were "helping the police with their inquiries" and I panicked, thinking that because Bob had called in the police only this morning, that they would arrest you. So I quickly thought up the lie. I hope none of it gets in the papers, or you might lose your job in the Civil Service.'

'I'm not in the Civil Service. I'm a policeman from Lochdubh in Sutherland, where I'm the local bobby.'

She stopped the car a little way away from the boarding-house and turned to him, the lights from the dashboard shining on her glasses, which she had put on to drive. 'You're a WHAT?'

'A policeman.'

'But you're not like any policeman I've ever met.'

'Have you met many?'

'No, but . . .'

'We come in all shapes and sizes.'

'So there was no need for me to lie?'

'Well, the fact that I am a policeman and I'm not in favour at the moment with my superiors might have made them keep me in all night. But honesty is always the best policy in a police investigation,' said Hamish, piously fighting down memories of the many times he had been economical with the truth. Miss Gunnery let in the clutch and moved off. 'The press are outside,' she said as a small group at the boarding-house gate appeared in the headlamps.

'Mostly local chaps,' commented Hamish, casting an expert eye over them.

'How can you tell?'

'The way they dress. Here goes. Just say "No comment yet" in as nice a voice as possible.'

They ran the press gauntlet. Emett, the policeman, was on guard outside the door. He stood aside and let them pass, his cold eyes fastening on Hamish as he did so.

They looked in the lounge but the rest had apparently gone to their rooms.

Hamish was suddenly weary. What a holiday! He said a firm goodnight to Miss Gunnery and shut the door of his room on her with a feeling of relief.

He sat down on the bed and started to remove his shoes. It was then, with one shoe half off, that he suddenly realized that although Miss Gunnery had given *him* an alibi, by accepting her lie and going along with it, he had supplied *her* with a cast-iron alibi.

And he was convinced someone in this boarding-house had murdered Bob Harris.

When he went down to the dining room in the morning, Cheryl and Tracey were there, both heavily made up and both wearing those short leather skirts and plunging tops.

'Going to a party?' asked Hamish.

Cheryl shrugged. 'Thon policeman says we werenae tae speak tae the press but Tracey and me want our photos in the papers. The minute we've had our breakfasts, we're goin't oot there.'

Andrew came into the room at that moment. He had dark shadows under his eyes, as if he had slept badly. He had just sat down when Doris arrived. She looked around the room with bleak, empty eyes and then, after a little hesitation, went and joined Andrew at his table. Then came the Brett family, the children wide-eyed and subdued.

'You're a policeman,' said Dermott, stopping at Hamish's table. It was a statement, not a question.

'That Crick told me,' Dermott went on. 'So what are you going to do about this?'

'I'm on holiday,' said Hamish, 'and I'm still a suspect myself, so I can't interfere.'

Mr and Mrs Rogers came into the dining room carrying plates of fried haggis and watery eggs. 'Has it occurred to you,' pursued Dermott, 'that one of us might have done it?'

Mrs Rogers was carrying three plates. She dropped them with a crash.

'Look,' said Hamish, 'that was the first thought about it I had. But just think. Which one of us here had a reason to murder Bob Harris?' All eyes slid to Doris.

'Yes, I know the wife's the first suspect, but can anyone see Doris actually killing anyone?'

Andrew's voice was hard. 'Drop it, Hamish. Doris has enough to bear without having to listen to all this.'

Hamish and Dermott murmured apologies. Dermott joined June and the children. Mrs Rogers scurried about cleaning up the mess. 'Some of you will just have to do without haggis,' said Mr Rogers.

'I think we could all do with a decent breakfast.' Hamish got to his feet. 'I'll cook it.'

'No one is allowed in the kitchen this morning,' exclaimed Mr Rogers, barring the doorway.

'Then it's time they were,' said Miss Gunnery. 'Come along, Hamish. I'll help you.'

Despite the Rogerses' protests, they collected up the plates that had been served, and walked through to the kitchen, where they scraped the contents into the rubbish bin. Hamish picked up a pot and took it over to the sink and washed it thoroughly. He began to scramble eggs while Miss Gunnery made piles of toast.

It was voted the best breakfast they had ever had and was eaten deaf to the speech made by Mr Rogers that they would all have to pay for the extra eggs.

'Put on the radio over there,' said Dermott, 'and let's hear the news.'

Hamish looked anxiously at Doris. 'Do you think you can stand it?'

She nodded. Andrew reached across the table and took her hand and pressed it.

Hamish switched on an old-fashioned radio in the corner, the kind featured in old war documentaries with families listening to Churchill talking about fighting them on the beaches. It crackled into life in time for the nine o'clock news. 'Police have discovered the remains of three bodies in the garden of a house in Tanwill Road, Perth,' said the announcer. 'The house belongs to a builder, Frank Duffy. The area has been cordoned off and police are appealing to the public to stay away. We will bring you an update as soon as we have further news. An IRA attack on Heathrow Airport was foiled when . . .' And so the news went on without a single mention of Bob Harris.

'Have the police here asked for press silence on our murder?' asked Dermott.

Hamish switched off the radio and sat down again. 'A man being hit on the head and pushed into the water is as nothing compared to these Perth murders. The only reason there were so many press around last night was because there was nothing much else going on. At least it means we'll get peace and quiet today.'

'Whit?' Cheryl and Tracey looked at Hamish in comic dismay. 'Whit about us? We want our photos in the papers.' Cheryl went to the window and looked out. 'Not a soul,' she said in disgust. 'And we got up at dawn tae get ready.'

'I think we are forgetting our manners,' said Miss Gunnery severely. 'Doris, I am sure you know you have our deepest sympathy.' This statement was followed by rather shamefaced murmurs all round. And yet it was hard to feel sorry for Doris. She was now free of a dreadful husband.

'A police car's jist arrived,' said Cheryl, still looking out.

After a few moments the door of the dining room opened and Deacon came in. 'Tracey Fink and Cheryl Gamble,' he said, 'I must ask you to accompany us to the police station.'

'It's a fit-up. You cannae pin this one on us,' said Cheryl, whose home in Glasgow had satellite television.

'You were heard by some of the lads at the dance saying as how ye would like tae bump someone off tae see whit it felt like,' said Deacon. 'Come along. Ye've a lot of explaining to do.' He turned to Hamish. 'And I haven't finished with you by a long chalk. None of the rest of you leave Skag without permission.'

Protesting their innocence, Cheryl and Tracey were led out.

'I think we'd all feel more at ease with each other,' said Hamish into the following silence, 'if we all got together and said where we were yesterday afternoon. Bob Harris was seen at two o'clock on the jetty by that fisherman and he says when he looked out half an hour later, there was no sign of Harris. So if we move through to the lounge, we could explain to each other where we all were at that time.'

'And I think Doris has just as much as she can take at the moment,' protested Andrew.

But Doris said in a small voice, 'Don't you see, we've got to know? I don't mind.'

And so they all went through to the lounge and sat round in a circle.

'Maybe we'll start with Doris and let her get it over with,' said Hamish.

In a flat voice, Doris described her day. 'I knew Bob was livid with me over protecting Hamish. I was terrified. I had never really stood up to him before. So I simply ran away. I did not go into Skag. I went the other way, along the empty beach. I walked miles. I didn't have any lunch and I turned back and began to think that even this boarding-house tea might be bearable. I knew I had to face Bob sometime or other and suddenly I wanted to get it over with. There's no point asking for witnesses. There weren't any. I didn't come across anyone.'

'I'll go next,' said Andrew. 'I went after Doris. But I thought she might have gone to Skag. I went into a shop around lunch-time and bought a sausage roll and a carton of orange juice and sat on the bench outside and ate them. I didn't want to come back here. I wanted some time to myself. The shopkeeper should remember me, but the murder happened later. I didn't go near the jetty. I was beginning to hate this place. The only reason I came here was because it was cheap. I lost a lot of money on a stupid business venture after

I was made redundant from the army. I began to wonder what I was doing in the wilds of Scotland in a seedy boarding-house. I hated Harris. I'm glad he's dead, but I didn't kill him. Someone must have seen me, apart from that shopkeeper. In the afternoon, I walked a little way out of Skag in the direction of the town. Cars passed me on the road, but as I didn't know a murder was taking place, I didn't take note of licence plates or anything like that. Then, because most of Skag is on the dole, I think the residents who were not at the fair were indoors watching soaps on television. That's all I have to say.'

Hamish looked at Dermott. 'Were you all together yesterday?' he asked.

'Yes, we went into Skag and bought stuff for a picnic and took the kids to the beach,' said Dermott, 'just along from the boarding-house. We were there all day.'

Hamish's sharp eyes noticed the way the children sat very still and quiet and how June looked steadily at the floor. He's lying, he thought suddenly. Instead he said aloud, 'Did anyone see you?'

'Mr Rogers might have seen us. He came out just after lunch-time and got in his car and drove off in the direction of Skag. I saw him through my binoculars.'

'Miss Gunnery?'

'I seem to have had the same uneventful day as the rest of you,' said the schoolteacher. 'I went for a walk into Skag after lunch-time. I was getting bored. I thought I would see some of you in the village. I took a look around and then came back here and sat in my room and read a book. When you didn't come back, Hamish, I took the key to your room and then took Towser out for a walk.'

Obviously, thought Hamish, the police had not told the others of Miss Gunnery's tale of sleeping with him. He had a sudden longing for his own police station and his own phone. If one of these people had murdered Bob Harris and that someone was not his wife, then there might be a clue in their backgrounds.

He stood up abruptly. He wanted to get away by himself. There were Mr and Mrs Rogers still to question, but they could wait.

'It looks as if not one of us has a decent alibi,' he said, standing up. 'I'm going for a walk.'

'I'll come with you.' Miss Gunnery got up as well.

'Not this time,' said Hamish. 'I want to think.'

'Sit down, Hamish,' said Andrew sharply. 'We haven't heard your story.'

'Sorry,' said Hamish, feeling sheepish. 'I forgot I wasn't on duty. I went into Skag. I bought a couple of books and spent the day reading them on a bank of the river on the far side of

Skag. I don't know if anyone saw me. You see, people in Skag don't know who we are and they wouldn't have bothered to take any particular notice of any of us, them not knowing there was going to be a murder. Then around tea-time, I went and bought a fish supper and took it to the jetty to eat. I finished it and went to look over the edge of the water. That's when I saw Harris. I tried to revive him even though I was pretty sure he was stone-dead. Sorry, Doris.'

'But why should the police think you a suspect when you're a policeman yourself?' asked Dermott. 'And considering you were trying to save the man?'

'During the questioning, Deacon told me that they thought I had dragged the body clear to cover any clues and then had tried to revive Harris to throw them off the scent. I'll go for a walk and see if I can think of something.'

Hamish collected Towser and went outside. 'Where are you going?' demanded Crick, who had replaced Emett to take over guarding the boarding-house. 'We havenae finished with you.'

'I'll be back,' said Hamish. 'I'm chust taking my dog along the beach for a bit.'

'Well, see you don't go far,' said Crick sourly.

Hamish walked sadly away. Not only had the local police found out that he had been demoted from sergeant but that he was the type of man who seduced otherwise respectable spinsters, for Miss Gunnery, even with a layer of make-up, always succeeded in looking just what she was, a retired unmarried schoolteacher.

With Towser loping at his heels, he walked away along the beach. Pink shells sparkled in the blowing white sand and the wind had risen again. The waves were choppy, blown blue and black with fretting white caps. A sun-blackened piece of seaweed blew against his legs.

He sat down and considered the case. As it stood at the moment, the only one with a motive was Doris. It was a crime which could have been committed on the spur of the moment. There was Bob looking down into the water. A piece of wood lying handy. One quick blow to the head in a fit of rage and murder was done. But Doris did not look the impulsive type. He was sure that she would think too much about the action to perform it. She would think that before she struck him he might turn round. She would think about the consequences. Still, he did not know Doris very well. What if she had fallen in love for the first time and with Andrew Biggar? What if they had planned the murder between them? And what was he to do about Miss Gunnery's alibi?

He had allowed her to lie to the police. But if he told them she had been lying, they might well charge her with obstructing the police in their inquiries. And while he was on the subject of lying, Dermott had most certainly been lying. The children had been told not to say anything. But why on earth would Dermott want to murder a double-glazing salesman? Wait a bit. They had met before. Dermott had been at the boarding-house before when Bob Harris had been there. It had been owned by a couple of women, the Misses Blane, that was it. They had retired to a house in Skag. He would take Towser back and tell Crick he was going into town for lunch. And he might as well call round at the police station and see if he could find out what they were doing with Cheryl and Tracey. He could not believe for a minute that the couple had done murder for kicks. Still, it might be a good idea to find out if either of them had a criminal record.

Priscilla Halburton-Smythe was staying with an old school friend at her family mansion outside Chipping Norton in Gloucestershire. She was enjoying a late leisurely breakfast. She had read *The Times* and the *Daily Telegraph*. She now picked up a copy of the *Daily Bugle* and idly turned over the pages, stopping suddenly as the face of Hamish Macbeth stared up at her under a headline of MAN MURDERED AND THROWN INTO SEA, the gentlemen of the press considering a body in the sea more exciting than one in a river. She read it carefully. The caption under the photograph merely stated: 'Mr Hamish Macbeth and Miss Felicity Gunnery leaving the police station in Skag by car after helping police with their inquiries.' In the story, it listed the residents at the boarding-house, and among them were the names of Hamish Macbeth and Miss Gunnery. The flash photograph had been kind to Miss Gunnery's heavily made-up face. To Priscilla it was all too clear. Hamish had taken a holiday in Skag with this Felicity Gunnery. And to think she had occasionally thought about him and wondered what he was doing!

Chapter Four

Oh, thou demon Drink, thou fell destroyer;
Thou curse of society, and its greatest annoyer.
What hast thou done to society, let me think?
I answer thou hast caused the most of ills, thou demon Drink.

– William McGonagall

After having left Towser at the boarding-house, with the plea to Miss Gunnery to take the dog out for a walk if he was not back until late, Hamish set out for the village. He had to find the Misses Blane and he also had to find someone friendly to him in the police inquiry. He wondered whether he would find anyone at all. No doubt it was all round those involved in the murder inquiry that he was a womanizer, a failed policeman and a suspect.

He went to the post office, or rather sub-post office, a hatch at the back of the Asian store, and asked for the voters' roll. He slid his finger rapidly down the names until he located

Blane. The address was Glebe Street, near the Church of Scotland.

He made his way there and ended up outside one of the thatched cottages which crouched at the end of Glebe Street like old shaggy animals. Seagulls screamed and wheeled mournfully overhead. He rapped at the polished brass knocker and waited. After some moments, he heard shuffling footsteps. Then the door opened and an elderly woman with a toad-like face peered up at him. 'What do you want? I'm not buying anything.'

'I'm not selling anything,' said Hamish amiably. He smiled at her. 'It is one of the Misses Blane, is it not?'

'I'm Elizabeth Blane. Only one of us. Nancy died last month.'

'I wanted to ask you about The Friendly House.'

Her eyes gleamed behind her thick spectacles. 'Making a mess of it, are they? Good. Come in.'

He followed her into a dark parlour. A squat woman with sparse grey hair and a yellowish skin, she walked leaning heavily on a stick. She kept running her tongue over her pale, thick lips, looking more than ever like a toad in search of a juicy fly.

'Murder,' she said with satisfaction. 'I knew they'd make a mess of it. But this is better than I hoped.'

Hamish sat down opposite her, wondering why she had not asked who he was or why he had come to see her.

'Why did you think the Rogerses would make a mess of it?'

'Me and Nancy ran a good house, good food, nice rooms. We tried to train Rogers in our ways. But he said he could make a fortune by cutting prices and cutting costs, more fool him. Cocky idiot.'

'So why did you sell to him?'

'Nobody else wanted it. We were getting too old to cope. So Harris is dead. Well, that's hardly a surprise. I suppose Brett did him in.'

'Dermott Brett? Why on earth him?'

'Oh, because of that scene last year. Yes, we ran that place like clockwork, me and Nancy. My scones are still a legend in Skag. Did you hear about my scones?'

'Not yet. What was the scene about?'

'Brett's wife turned up for the day, so that June, who calls herself his wife, had to make herself scarce and take the children with her. Me and Nancy didn't rat on Brett, but as soon as his wife had left, we told him we were having nothing of that sort here and he would have to go. Harris jeered at him and said he would tell his wife that he was spending his holidays with another woman.'

'But Dermott Brett said he didn't know the boarding-house was under new management, so if he thought it was still you and your sister, why did he come back?'

'That's havers. He knew we were selling all right because we told him we were putting the place on the market at the end of the season.'

Hamish sat thinking. Dermott had said he and 'his family' had been on the beach at the time of the murder and that Rogers might have seen him. But the beach was a quarter of a mile from the boarding-house, across the dunes, and then shielded by that bank of shingle. How could Dermott even have caught a glimpse of Rogers through binoculars, and there was no way that Rogers could have seen him.

'Who are you?' demanded Miss Blane.

'I'm a policeman.'

'Why aren't you in uniform?'

'Because I am on holiday, but I happen to be staying at the boarding-house and –'

'You're the one that was helping the police with their inquiries.'

'Well,' lied Hamish, 'the press put it that way. As a matter o' fact, I'm helping with the investigation.'

'At least you had the courtesy to call. I thought the police would have been round here right away.'

'Have any of the others been at the boarding-house before? There's a Miss Gunnery, a retired schoolteacher, a Mr Andrew

Biggar, ex-army man, and two lassies from Glasgow, Cheryl Fink and Tracey Gamble.'

'Not that I recall.'

'Did Rogers meet Harris and Brett last year?'

'No, we didn't negotiate with Rogers until the end of the summer.'

'I wonder why he came back,' said Hamish, half to himself. 'He's obviously worried about being found out, and yet he came back. And it's not really very much like living in sin when you turn up with a woman and her three children. And the children call him "Daddy".'

'Maybe he is,' said Miss Blane cynically. 'I don't know what the world is coming to. I remember when this was a nice village, with decent people, and the people who came in the summer were nice ordinary people as well. Now it's all drink and worse. In my day the teenagers didn't have enough money to drink. Aye, and they had to work. *And* they showed respect to their elders.' Her voice had a whining, grating edge. The room was small and stuffy and crowded with tables cluttered with photos and china ornaments. There were lace curtains at the windows which let in very little light.

It all felt claustrophobic. He rose to go. 'You'll stay for a cup of tea,' she said. Naked loneliness suddenly looked out of her eyes. Of course she was lonely, Hamish thought, nasty old bat. But he sat down again. One day he might be old and nasty, too.

So he patiently listened to her complaints while he drank tea and agreed that her scones were the best in the world. She complained first about the village, then about the government, then about the European Community, then about the way America was being run, and when she reached the forthcoming independence of Hong Kong, Hamish felt he had had enough. He took his leave, promising to call again.

Outside, he took a deep breath of sandy, salty air. His best plan now would be to stroll past the police station and see if any of the police looked friendly. He stopped at the church notice-board opposite the police station and pretended to read, twisting round every now and then to watch the comings and goings. And then he saw a smart little policewoman arriving in a patrol car. He waited, wondering if she might be going off duty. After half an hour, she emerged in a blouse and trousers and headed in the direction of the pub. Hamish followed. He waited until he saw her going into the pub and then went in himself.

She was standing at the bar, sipping a gin and tonic. Hamish stood beside her and ordered a whisky. He turned and smiled down at her. 'Cheers, Constable,' he said, raising his glass.

'Cheers,' she said, studying him. She saw a tall, thin man with an engaging face and hazel eyes. His red hair had a natural wave and shone in the dim light of the pub.

'I'm a copper as well,' said Hamish. She had a pert little face, small eyes, small nose, small mouth, and a quantity of shiny, curly fair hair and what Hamish thought of as an old-fashioned body: rounded bust, tiny waist and generous hips.

Her eyes took on a hard, suspicious look. 'You're Hamish Macbeth,' she said.

'Aye, that iss right. Suspect number one.'

Her face relaxed a bit. Hamish looked so inoffensive. 'Did you do it?'

'Murder Harris to enliven the boredom of my holiday? No.'

'You just stick to seducing the ladies.'

He silently cursed Miss Gunnery. 'As to that,' he said, 'I might tell you something about the case if you're interested.'

'I am interested. I would like to have more to do with it. I'm from Dungarton and my job is to do all the dogsbody work. That Deacon even asked me to make the tea.'

'Neffer!'

'Aye. Treats me like a secretary.'

'What's your name?'

'Maggie Donald.'

'You're not from these parts?'

'No, Fife. I came up here to live with my auntie when my parents died.'

'Let me get you another drink,' said Hamish, 'and we'll sit over there and have a wee chat.'

'As long as you're going to talk about the case and not chat me up.'

Hamish looked at her severely. 'Well,' she said defensively, 'you *have* earned yourself a bit of a reputation.'

He bought them a drink each and carried them over to a table in the corner. The pub was quiet. Apart from them, there were only two seedy-looking youths over at the fruit machine.

'So,' said Maggie, 'who do you think did it?'

'I would have thought the wife was the obvious choice,' said Hamish. 'The man was a nag. He made her life a misery. Then along comes this Andrew Biggar and I think that pair are falling in love. But Andrew seems a decent fellow, and Doris is so meek and mild, and she was terrified of her husband. I can't see her biffing him on the head.'

'What about the fascinating Miss Gunnery? Did she know Hamish before?'

He shook his head. 'Look, I'll tell you something about me and Miss Gunnery if you promise not to repeat it.'

'I can't promise that in case it turns out to have any bearing on the case.'

'No, it hasn't. Can you see me coming all the way from Lochdubh to murder a man I don't know? Miss Gunnery, in a mistaken attempt to save me from being charged with murder, or that was the way she saw it, got herself up like a tart and told those gullible detectives that I had spent the afternoon in bed wi' her.'

'And had you?'

'No.'

'But you should have told Deacon! That's obstructing the police in –'

'I know all that,' he interrupted impatiently. 'I wass fed up wi' the row I had that morning, what with Harris calling the police and accusing me of assaulting him. I went off and bought a couple of paperbacks in the village and went out to that bend of the river on the Dungarton side of the village and read all day. Then I bought a fish supper and took it to the harbour to eat it. That's when I found Harris.'

'And you expect me to keep quiet about Miss Gunnery's lie?'

'Yes.'

'Why?'

'Because you want to get in on this case. Because I am living at the boarding-house. Because I know the people concerned.'

'I can't promise. But I would like to know a bit more about them. Deacon has pulled in those two young girls.'

'Why did he do that?' asked Hamish. 'I mean, they were evidently shooting their mouths off at the dance about how they would like to murder someone for kicks, but surely that isn't enough to make them suspects.'

'Cheryl has form.'

'What kind of form?'

'GBH.'

'Grievous bodily harm! And her so young. She must be about nineteen at the oldest.'

'She's twenty. She cut someone's face with a bottle two years ago at a Glasgow dance hall. A drunken row. Cheryl thought the other girl was stealing her boyfriend. She met Tracey in prison.'

'And what was Tracey in for?'

'She did a short sentence for shoplifting. She was sent to prison because it was her fifth offence.'

'I'm slipping,' said Hamish, shaking his head ruefully. 'I would haff said they were chust a pair of regular young girls who wore silly clothes and too much make-up.'

'So what do you know?' asked Maggie.

Hamish settled down and told her the alibis of the residents, some of which she had already heard from her colleagues. It was when he got to Doris's alibi that he suddenly stiffened. 'Wait a bit,' he said. 'Doris told me and the others that she had walked away from the village along the beach the day of the murder. But I saw her myself walking towards the village. Why did she lie?'

'Perhaps she and this Andrew planned the murder together,' said Maggie. 'It keeps coming back to her somehow.'

'I certainly don't want to believe it, because they are nice people.' Hamish tilted his whisky this way and that in his glass. 'I can't imagine either of them murdering anyone.'

'It happens,' said Maggie. 'Think of it – years of bullying building up resentment after resentment in Doris's mind, and then she falls for this Andrew. Light the blue paper and retire. She might have gone up like a rocket, seen him standing right at the edge of the jetty and *bam!* into the water goes one very dead husband. And why did Doris lie to you about which way she went when she left the hotel?'

'I'll find out. What did she tell the police?'

'I'll need to look at the statements. I tell you what, I'm working until seven this evening. I'd better not be seen with you. If you start walking from the boarding-house just before seven, on the road, not the beach, I'll pick you up and we'll go somewhere and talk and share notes.'

'Right, Maggie. Can I get you another drink?'

She shook her head. 'I've had my limit. It's a good thing I'm slimming. I haven't had anything to eat. Off with you before any of the coppers come in and find me talking to you.'

Hamish left feeling pleased with his morning's work. He realized he was hungry and should have eaten something in the pub. He waited until Maggie left and then went back in and ordered some tired-looking sandwiches and a glass of ginger beer. He returned to the boarding-house by way of the beach and met Miss Gunnery walking Towser.

'What's happening?' he asked.

'You're to report to the police station, Hamish,' she said wearily. Her hair was once more scraped back and the pale light from the grey sea and milky sky reflected on her gold-rimmed glasses and gave her a blind look. 'They've been questioning and questioning. Me and the Bretts, Andrew and Doris, and the Rogerses. They even had a word with the children, especially Heather. That boatman is a menace. He told them all about Heather discussing ways to make murder look like an accident.'

'I'd best be off then.' Hamish stooped and patted Towser. 'You'd best go home with Miss Gunnery like a good boy. I'll get you some ham.' He waved to Miss Gunnery and set off back to Skag.

At the police station, he caught a glimpse of Maggie. She was carrying a tray of dirty teacups. He was ushered into the interview room again to face Deacon and Clay.

'So you and that Miss Gunnery were lying,' began Deacon.

With all his heart, Hamish cursed the fickle Maggie.

But he folded his arms and faced them in silence. 'You should be mair careful who you tell secrets to,' jeered Clay.

'So why am I here alone?' demanded Hamish suddenly. 'Surely you should haff pulled Miss Gunnery in as well.'

'Give us time,' said Deacon sourly. 'So where were you, laddie?'

Hamish told them slowly and carefully how he had spent his day, ending up with an exasperated cry of 'If I had murdered the man, I would haff left the body where it wass for somebody else to find.'

'Aye, maybe,' said Deacon surprisingly. 'We've been doing a bit more checking up on you. Some detective over at Strathbane, Jimmy Anderson, phoned to say we shouldnae give you a hard time, for you're a dab hand at solving cases and letting your superiors take the credit.'

Hamish said nothing.

'And it is our opinion, having also checked on Miss Gunnery and found out she is who she says, a schoolteacher who took early retirement and one with an unblemished reputation, that we'll leave you where you are, Hamish Macbeth, because you could be very useful to us. Now, Maggie tells us that what worries you about the wife, Mrs Doris Harris, is that she told you she was on the other side of the beach, away from Skag, on the day of the murder, and yet you yourself saw her heading towards the village.'

'Yes,' said Hamish bleakly, thinking women were the devil in general and Maggie in particular.

'But we took statements from the Brett children, or rather from the eldest, Heather, and she says she wandered off from her parents and saw Doris in the distance, exactly where she said she was.'

'I'm not mistaken,' said Hamish firmly. 'I definitely saw Doris on the road to Skag that morning. Why should Heather lie? Since Maggie's been shooting off her mouth all round, I may as well tell you that Dermott Brett and June are not married.' He paused for a moment, remembering that he had not told Maggie about the Bretts. 'There was a scene last year when Dermott's wife turned up. June and the children went off somewhere, but the Misses Blane, who owned the boarding-house then, told him they would have nothing of that kind under their respectable roof. Now Dermott told me that he did not know the boarding-house was under new management, but the surviving Miss Blane told me today that he was well aware of the fact that they meant to sell up at the end of the summer.'

'We'd better question them all again,' said Deacon heavily. 'You've been busy.'

'I'm there,' said Hamish simply. 'What about those two, Cheryl and Tracey?'

'We've put the wind up them. Couple of young slags. They're silly and dangerous when they're on the booze but pretty harmless off it. Keep an eye on them.'

'You mean you want me to work with you?' asked Hamish.

'May as well. You're a copper. But no withholding any evidence or having silly biddies who ought to know better say you were in bed with them. So let's go over it from the beginning again, Macbeth, and tell us all you know about them.'

So Hamish told every detail, right from the search of his suitcase through the day of the murder and what he had found out that day.

Deacon studied him with shrewd eyes while Hamish spoke. He was an odd fellow, thought Deacon. His voice was less sibilant than when he had first come in but still had a pleasant Highland lilt. His hazel eyes betrayed nothing of what he was really thinking as he spoke. Actually Hamish was experiencing an uncomfortable feeling of betrayal. The unfortunate residents of the boarding-house had become his friends in such a short time. He pictured them all as he spoke: pleasant Andrew Biggar and vulnerable Doris, dependable Miss Gunnery and the Brett family, and he still thought of them as a family, even the dreadful Cheryl and Tracey. How happy they had all been when they went to the fair. Not for the first time, he felt queasy about his job. But, his thoughts ran on, as his voice delivered the report in calm, measured tones, he could not protect a murderer. That was the one thing that had carried him firmly through several nasty murder cases – taking of life was wrong. No one had the right to snuff out even such a repulsive character as Bob Harris.

'Well, we'll pull in Dermott Brett for questioning first thing tomorrow,' said Deacon when Hamish had finished.

'What was the final result of the pathologist's report?' asked Hamish.

'Stunned by a blow to the head from, possibly, a piece of driftwood, and then died from drowning. Given an element of surprise and a heavy piece of wood, any of them could have done it, but the one thing in Doris Harris's favour is that the blow was struck by someone the same height as Harris, or so we guess, and Harris was five feet ten and Doris is about five feet two inches.'

Hamish looked at both detectives sadly. 'The boatman was the last to see him, and then he was standing, but had Bob Harris been drinking a lot?'

'Like a fish,' said Deacon.

'After the boatman saw him, he might have been sitting down, with his legs over the edge. Anyone then could have struck him hard and toppled him over.'

'Good point,' said Deacon and Hamish felt like a rat. He had successfully put them all back in the frame.

'That'll be all for now, Macbeth. Off wi' you and let us know how you get on.'

Hamish wanted to protest he was on holiday, that he did not want to have anything more to do with it, but he was suddenly desperate to get out of the stuffy room and away from the tantalizing smell of Clay's cigarettes.

He nodded to both of them and went out. Maggie was crossing the entrance hall. 'Hamish,' she began.

'Leave me alone,' he snapped. He shouldered his way past her and went out.

The day was full of sun and wind and movement. White sand glittering with specks of mica danced crazily through the streets. The calm grey of the morning had gone. Seagulls wheeled and dipped and screamed overhead. Children's voices were carried on the wind, along with snatches of music from the fairground. There were smells of frying fish and chips – that shop never seemed to close – smells of salt water and tar, and smells from the fairground of hot oil, candy-floss and onions and hot dogs.

He went to the Asian store and bought a packet of cold ham for Towser. Then he reluctantly made his way back along the beach through the blowing sand and wheeling gulls to the point where he cut off inland over the shingle and over the dunes to the boarding-house.

He looked at his watch. Time for tea. What dreadful menu had the Rogerses thought up? And why did they, the guests, not complain more about it? Americans, say, would not have put up with such food for a moment, no matter how cheap the price.

He fed Towser the ham and then went down to the dining room, blinking a little in surprise as he realized they were all there. Cheryl and Tracey were subdued and their eyes red with recent weeping. He felt sorry for them and then reminded himself sternly that they were ex-criminals.

He sat down heavily opposite Miss Gunnery. 'How did it go?' she asked anxiously.

'They know you were lying about being with me that afternoon,' said Hamish.

'How?'

'I told them,' said Hamish, too weary to explain how one policewoman had betrayed them. 'It doesn't do any good to lie. I'm grateful to you, but there wass no need for you to put your reputation on the line for me. You can't cover up things in a murder case.'

'But surely the police are stupid sometimes. Deacon did not strike me as a particularly intelligent man.'

'He's hardly an academic, but I know the kind, solid and plodding, and they get there in the end.'

Miss Gunnery glanced over at Doris. 'I hope Doris is all right. She's looking awfully strained.'

'She'll still be suffering from shock,' said Hamish. 'Oh, God, what's this?'

He poked his fork at the mess on his plate. It was some sort of beef covered in an ersatz brown gravy. But it smelt bad. It smelt *rank*. Hamish looked around the dining room. He raised his voice. 'Have any of you eaten any of this?'

'Just a little,' said Dermott gloomily. 'That's all I could manage.'

Mr Rogers came into the dining room with his usual glazed smile. 'You can take our plates away,' said Hamish wrathfully. 'This meat is bad. Where do you get it from?'

'From the butcher's in Skag.'

'There isn't a butcher's in Skag.'

'I mean Dungarton.'

'Look here, Mr Rogers,' said Hamish. 'Enough is enough. Take this muck away and produce something edible or I'll report you to the tourist board *and* the health authorities.'

Rogers flashed Hamish a look of pure hatred, but he called his wife and together, in sulky silence, they took the plates away.

'Why did the police want to see you again, Hamish?' said Andrew.

'They weren't satisfied with my earlier statement,' said Hamish. 'I'm afraid we're all going to be questioned over and over again.'

'I cannae take ony mair,' wailed Cheryl. 'It's like the Gestapo.'

'It's murder,' said Hamish flatly. 'We're all in trouble until the murderer is found. I wonder where Rogers gets this filth he's been giving us.'

A bell sounded from the hall outside. Rogers appeared, looking flushed and bad-tempered. He went into the hall and soon reappeared. 'Someone to see you, Macbeth,' he announced.

'Mr Macbeth to you.' Hamish got up and went out to the hall. His face grew hard when he saw Maggie Donald standing there. 'What do you want?'

'Look, Hamish, I've come to apologize. It wasn't my fault.'

'Who else could haff told them the truth about Miss Gunnery?'

'It was the barman at the pub, Fred Allsopp. After we'd left, Clay came in for a drink and he told him I had been in and he described you. So Clay came back to the station and grilled me and said I was "consorting with a prime suspect" and my job was on the line, and I panicked.'

'I still don't see that's any excuse.' Hamish looked every bit as huffy as he felt.

'You don't know what it's like, being a woman.' Maggie looked at him pleadingly. 'The cards are stacked against you. Unless I play up to them, I'll be carrying trays of tea and doing traffic duty at Highland games for the rest of my career.' She smiled up at him tentatively and Hamish relented.

'All right then,' he said. 'I could do wi' someone who's not involved to discuss the case with.'

'Have you eaten?' asked Maggie.

'Not yet. Rogers produced some filth which I sent back. I'm waiting for the replacement.'

'I've got my car. As a peace offering, I'll take you to Dungarton for dinner.'

'Right, you're on. I'll get Miss Gunnery to look after Towser.'

When he returned to the dining room, they were all still waiting to be served. He told Miss Gunnery that he was going out to dinner with a policewoman and could she please take care of Towser. For a moment she looked sad and he felt obscurely guilty. 'Am I going to be arrested for lying?' she asked.

'No, as far as I know, nothing's going to happen to you,' said Hamish.

'You've joined them,' she said. 'You're not one of us any more.'

'It's my job.' Hamish looked down at her ruefully. Maggie came into the dining room. 'A car has arrived to take Mrs Harris to the police station.'

Doris stood up. 'Isn't she even going to be allowed to eat?' demanded Andrew angrily. 'I'm coming with you, Doris.'

They went out together.

'When you're ready, Hamish,' said Maggie.

'So that's your policewoman,' said Miss Gunnery, looking older and shrivelled somehow. She said half to herself, 'Sometimes I forget my age.'

Hamish, sad and somehow still feeling guilty, was glad to get away from the atmosphere of the dining room and its smells of bad food.

'I feel like a traitor,' he said as he and Maggie walked out together.

'All part of being in the police force,' said Maggie cheerfully. She was pleased. Deacon had told her that as Hamish Macbeth obviously fancied her – having jumped to the idea that the only interest Hamish could have in the young policewoman was carnal – she should stick close to him because, 'Macbeth is going to find out what he can for us, but I don't want him hiding any evidence.'

Maggie drove competently along the road to Dungarton. White sand whirled and danced in the sidelights. It never got dark enough on these northern summer evenings to put the full lights on. 'I'll be glad when this is over,' said Maggie. 'I'm beginning to feel I'm getting sand-blasted. The wretched stuff gets everywhere as well. What on earth brought you to a place like Skag for a holiday, Hamish?'

'I wanted a break,' said Hamish. 'It looked a pretty place in a magazine someone gave me. And it was cheap. You know a policeman's pay doesn't go very far. I feel now I should ha' been more adventurous, gone to a bucket-shop travel agency and risked one of those Spanish holidays and hoped they'd got around to building the hotel before I got there.'

'I went on one of those last year,' said Maggie. 'It was very good, and at least you know you've got a chance of fine weather. Mind you, it seemed odd to be all the way down in the south of Spain and surrounded by British. I don't think I met any Spanish apart from the staff at the hotel.'

'To get back to the case,' said Hamish, 'why are they pulling Doris in again?'

'Did you tell them about her going towards Skag when she said she went the other way?'

'Yes.'

'Well, that's no doubt why they want to see her. But little Heather swears she saw Doris where she said she was.'

'In order to see Doris,' said Hamish slowly, 'she would need to have wandered away from her parents – sorry, you'll find out if you don't know already that Dermott and June aren't married – but they both seem devoted to the children and I can't see either of them letting young Heather wander off by herself.'

'I heard about Dermott. They're checking into his background. Has his name appeared in the press yet?'

'I don't know. I haven't see all the newspapers. It's a shame,' he added. 'I can't help hoping it works out all right for them.'

'It won't work out all right if he's guilty of bumping off Harris to shut his mouth.'

They drove the rest of the way in silence until she pulled up outside an Indian restaurant in Dungarton. 'I hope you like curry,' said Maggie as they walked up the restaurant steps together.

'Anything's going to taste marvellous after the cooking at The Friendly House.'

As they ate, Hamish looked about the crowded restaurant. He never ceased to marvel at these Asians who came all the way to the north of Scotland to start a business, so very far from home. And thank God for that, he thought, as he ate his way steadily through a delicious lamb curry.

'I'd like to find out where Rogers gets his supplies from,' he said as he finally pushed his empty plate away.

'Maybe he's just a bad cook,' volunteered Maggie.

'No, there's more to it than that. That meat tonight was bad.'

'I think we're concentrating on too many suspects.' Maggie looked at him seriously. 'I think it was the wife. I mean, it usually is. No one else had any reason to kill him.'

'It wass an act of rage.' Hamish's voice, sibilant again, showed he was becoming upset. 'It could have been any one of them.'

Maggie's voice was gentle. 'I know you don't want it to be her.'

'Aye, that's a fact. But concentrating solely on Doris might make us miss someone else.' He fell silent as his mind ranged over the possibilities. He saw Tracey and Cheryl, giggling and laughing, coming across Bob Harris at the edge of the jetty and deciding on impulse to commit the murder they had so recently talked about committing for 'kicks'.

Then the picture faded to be replaced by one of Dermott, having left his 'family' on the beach, creeping forward with a piece of driftwood in his hand. After that came a bright image of Miss Gunnery whacking Harris on the head as efficiently as she would have whacked a pupil with a ruler in the old days of teaching. But that picture was immediately replaced by one of Doris again, a Doris driven mad with years of bullying and abuse.

'I haven't got down to questioning any of them properly,' said Hamish. 'I'll start tomorrow. What about you? Tell me about yourself. How long have you been in the police force?'

'Two years. I was teaching infants before then and I wanted a bit of excitement. It hasn't been all that exciting. Not what I expected. In these days of female equality, I didn't expect to be treated as some sort of servant by the men.'

'You're young and attractive,' said Hamish cynically. 'By the time this job has eaten into you, you'll begin to look like a hard old bat and then they won't even know the difference.'

She raised her glass of wine. 'I'll drink to that. Why are you in the police force, Hamish?'

'It suits me fine. It wass getting the police station at Lochdubh. Man, it's a lovely village.' He felt a sharp pang of homesickness. 'The people are nice and it's a gentle life.' He temporarily forgot about all the animosity against him. His eyes grew dreamy. 'Often when I hae a break, I chust stay at home in the police station, go fishing, and I've got a bit o' croft land up the back and some hens and ducks. We've had the murder or two, but, och, everything worked out chust fine.'

'I'd like to see Lochdubh,' said Maggie.

He smiled at her pert little face. 'Maybe you can pay me a visit when this is all over.'

'And do you think it will be?'

'It's got to be. There's a murderer in the middle o' us and I keep thinking that if we look at all the suspects the right way around, we'll have him . . . or her.'

'Tell me about some of your other cases,' Maggie said.

Although Hamish was not much given to talking about his exploits, he found it a relief to talk about other cases, other murders, and forget about the present tragedy.

It was nearly midnight when they finally left the restaurant and drove through the half-light. 'Quite suddenly it changes,' said Hamish. 'Soon the nights will be back again, and in the winter, there's only a few hours of light during the day.' Outside the boarding-house, he thanked her for dinner. 'My turn to take you out next time,' he said.

'What about tomorrow night?' asked Maggie.

'Aye, that would be fine, but I don't know this area, so I'll leave the choice of restaurant up to you.'

She gave him a swift kiss on the cheek, and feeling more light-hearted than he had felt since the murder, Hamish got out of the car, waved good night and went into the boarding-house. He made his way upstairs, planning to give Towser a last walk.

He unlocked the door of his bedroom and went inside. Towser lay stretched out on the bed. 'Come on, lazybones,' called Hamish.

The dog did not move. 'Come on, old boy.' Hamish walked up to him. He put his hand on Towser's rough coat and then went very still. Then he shook the dog.

He suddenly withdrew his shaking hand, a great black wave of misery engulfing him.

Towser was dead.

Chapter Five

There is sorrow enough in the natural way
From men and women to fill our day;
But when we are certain of sorrow in store,
Why do we always arrange for more?
Brothers and Sisters, I bid you beware
Of giving your heart to a dog to tear.
– Rudyard Kipling

Early the following morning, Maggie was summoned by Deacon.

'I want you to get along to that boarding-house and get hold of Macbeth.'

'Why, what's happened?'

'His dog's dead.'

Maggie stared. 'Did someone kill it?'

'The vet who was hauled out in the middle o' the night says it's natural causes. No autopsy necessary. The thing is, Macbeth wants to take the dead beastie back to Lochdubh to bury it. Did ye ever hear the like?'

Maggie shifted uncomfortably. 'He was probably fond of it. People get very fond of their pets.'

'But he's a policeman, lassie. And that wasnae even a police dog. Anyway, here's what we want you to do. We're giving you the day off. You're to get along there and offer to drive him home. I've found he has a habit of playing his cards close to his chest and I want to know everything he thinks.'

Maggie looked at him shrewdly. 'So he's as clever as that.'

'Aye, so I've been hearing. I'm not going to make the mistake of his superior over at Strathbane of under-estimating him. A murder crosses Macbeth's path and the murder is solved. But I don't want tae end up wi' egg all over my face because some visiting bobby's solved a case instead o' me. Get along wi' you. And get out o' that uniform first. Say it's your day off.'

'Yes, sir.' Maggie stood up, smoothing down her skirt. She did not feel anything for the loss of Hamish's dog. She was pleased to be in favour with Deacon and she was looking forward to an unexpected day off. 'Don't you think that Miss Gunnery might already have offered to run him?'

'If that's the case, tell the old bat she's wanted for further questioning and to stay put.'

She drove home to Dungarton, scrambled out of her uniform and into a pretty summer dress with short sleeves and a low neckline. Then she set out for Skag again, taking the coast road which led straight to the boarding-house.

They were all at breakfast when she walked into the dining room. The Brett children were sobbing. The death of Towser had affected them more than the murder. As she looked at Hamish's grim and set face, Maggie experienced a qualm of conscience. But it did not last long. 'I'm right sorry about your dog, Hamish,' she said. 'I have the day off. They told me at the station that you wanted to go over to Lochdubh. I'll be happy to drive you over.'

'I'm taking Mr Macbeth,' said Miss Gunnery, her eyes glinting through her glasses.

'I'm afraid that won't be possible, Miss Gunnery,' said Maggie. 'You will be called on for further questioning.' She turned round and faced the rest of them. 'That applies to the rest of you.'

'Whit a holiday!' cried Cheryl. Doris turned a trifle pale and Andrew took her hand and stared defiantly at Maggie.

'Oh, all right,' said Hamish ungraciously. 'I'll go and get the . . . body.'

Maggie went out and waited in the hall. Hamish came down with Towser's body wrapped in a tartan travelling rug which Miss Gunnery had given him. He nodded to Maggie. 'Let's go,' he said curtly.

As they drove off, Maggie said tentatively, 'I don't want to distress you further, Hamish, with speculation, but is the vet sure it was a natural death?'

'Yes.'

'How old was Towser?'

'Twelve.'

'That's a good age for a dog.'

Hamish stared bleakly out of the window and did not reply.

'Which way would you like to take?' asked Maggie. 'The new bridge over to Dornoch?'

'The Struie Pass and then Bonar Bridge, then Lairg.'

'Right you are. I've never been to Sutherland before.'

Hamish did not reply. Maggie switched on the radio. Moray Firth Radio sprang into life. The music of The Beatles filled the car.

Correctly judging that Hamish did not want to talk, Maggie drove steadily ever westward. She looked at the sky ahead and began to wish that she had put a sweater in the car, or even a raincoat. When they reached the viewpoint on the Struie Pass, Hamish said, 'That's Sutherland.'

Ahead of them lay range after range of mountains. The clouds above were cut by shafts of light, the kind William Blake has angels using as ladders. Maggie, not much given to sensitive feelings, none the less suppressed a little shiver. It was as if she were crossing the boundary into some weird savage land, so different from the tidy fields and towns of Fife, or the flat land around Dungarton in Moray. They stopped in Lairg for a bar lunch in the Sutherland Arms Hotel, hardly talking. Maggie was beginning to feel increasingly uncomfortable. She felt it was all a waste of time. Hamish, mourning his dead pet, was not going to talk about the case.

As she drove deeper into Sutherland under the shadow of the pillared mountains along a one-track road leading to the coast, Maggie found her voice. 'It looks as if it's getting cold, Hamish. Can you lend me a sweater when we get there?'

'Yes, I can find you something. No, don't turn off. Go straight towards Lochinver and then take the coast road north.'

'Far to go?'

'Not far now,' said Hamish.

The wind of Sutherland had begun to blow, tugging savagely at Maggie's small car, roaring across the sky above, sending ragged clouds streaming out above their heads.

She turned off at Lochinver and headed along a twisting coast road. The full force of the Atlantic thudded in on the rocky beach below the road. Weird twisted mountains reared up on the other side. A pair of buzzards cruised effortlessly on strong wings through the gale.

'That looks a posh place,' commented Maggie as she drove past the wrought-iron gates leading to Tommel Castle Hotel.

'Fairly pricey,' said Hamish, averting his eyes.

The one-track road plunged downhill again.

'Here's Lochdubh,' said Hamish.

Maggie drove over a picturesque hump-backed bridge. Lochdubh straggled along beside the sea loch of Lochdubh, whitewashed cottages, pretty gardens, a harbour with fishing boats riding at anchor on the choppy waves.

He directed her to the police station and told her to park at the side. He was just tenderly lifting Towser's dead body out of the back of the car when Mrs Wellington came bustling up.

'So you're back,' remarked the minister's wife. Maggie saw a large tweedy woman with a heavy face, a heavy bust, and an efficient air about her.

'I've come to bury my dog,' said Hamish flatly.

'Oh, Hamish,' said Mrs Wellington weakly. 'What happened?'

'Chust died. Chust like that,' said Hamish. 'I'm going to bury him up in the field at the back o' the station.'

'Now?'

'In about an hour. This is Policewoman Maggie Donald. Miss Donald, Mrs Wellington, the minister's wife.'

Maggie held out her hand, but Mrs Wellington did not seem to see it. Her large features were puckered up in distress as she watched Hamish carry the tartan rug-covered bundle out of the car. She turned abruptly and marched away. Hamish walked up the side of the house, and holding the bundle in one arm, fished in his pocket for the key and unlocked the door.

'I'll make us some coffee,' said Maggie. Her voice sounded too bright and hard in her own ears. 'Where's the cooker?'

'It's that stove over there. I'll light it in a minute.' Hamish walked through to the bedroom and laid Towser gently on the bed.

He came back into the kitchen and handed Maggie a sweater which she gratefully pulled on. He took kindling and newspaper from a basket next to the stove and got to work. Then, when the stove was roaring away, he put the kettle on the top. 'It won't take long,' he said. 'I'd better check my machine for messages.'

He went off into the office part of the station. Maggie opened cupboard doors until she found the one with cups and a jar of instant coffee. 'No milk,' she called.

'There's a box of powdered milk on the counter,' Hamish shouted back.

When the kettle boiled, Maggie made a couple of mugs of coffee. Hamish reappeared and sat down heavily. 'Nothing much to worry about on the machine,' he said. 'It's been nice and quiet. I phoned Sergeant Macgregor at Cnothan – him that's covering for me – and he says nothing at all has been happening.'

He pushed the cup of coffee away from him. 'I think I'll go up back and dig the grave. I cannae relax until this is over. No, you stay here,' he added quickly as Maggie rose to her feet. 'There's a television in the living room if you want to watch anything.'

'All right,' said Maggie awkwardly.

When he had gone, she carried her coffee-mug through to the living room and looked curiously around. There were a few battered chairs, a worn Wilton carpet, a bookshelf crammed with paperbacks, a stand full of sticks, crooks and fishing-rods, a good painting over the fireplace of a Highland scene, and a table at the window piled high with official papers and forms that had found their way from the cluttered office next door. There were some photographs on the mantelpiece. She studied them, cradling the cup in her hands. There was a family group, Hamish in the forefront, all of them with red hair like his. Then there was a photograph of Hamish standing on the waterfront beside a beautiful and elegant blonde. He had his arm around her and both looked radiantly happy. There was another of Hamish in a deck chair outside the police station, fast asleep.

She switched on the television set and sat down wondering who the beautiful blonde was. Was this the fiancée she had heard he had ditched?

There was a discussion on BBC 1 over the correct use of condoms. She stood up again – there was no remote control – and switched channels until she found an old black-and-white movie with Cary Grant and settled down to watch it.

After some time, she became aware of voices, cars arriving, noise and movement outside. She switched off the television set and went to the kitchen door and opened it.

Villagers were filing past in a long line. Round the back of the house they went and up to the field. She backed away from the door as Hamish appeared. He did not say anything. He went through to the bedroom and picked up the bundle that was Towser and went out again. After a few moments, she followed him.

Surely the whole village was there, she thought, startled, as she set off up the hill after him. Silent men and women stood around the grave Hamish had dug. The men were even wearing their 'best' suits, the tight old-fashioned ones they took out of mothballs for weddings and funerals. She tried to find it ridiculous, that a whole village should turn out for the funeral of one mongrel, but there was something imposing in the scene. The ragged clouds flew overhead, whipping at the women's scarves and skirts. The solemn faces seemed to belong to an older time. She could see the minister at the edge of the grave in his black suit and dog collar. Surely he was not going to read the burial service.

She joined the crowd around the grave but could not see anything because of the press of people and so she moved a little way up the hill and looked down on the scene. Hamish laid Towser in his tartan covering tenderly in the grave. Maggie thought it a waste of a good travelling-rug. He dropped some earth on the top. The minister, Mr Wellington, addressed the crowd. 'I am sure our hearts go out to Hamish on the sad death of his pet. The dog has often been called man's best friend, and Towser was a good example of this. May the Good Lord comfort you in your loss, Hamish. Let us pray.'

To Maggie's acute embarrassment, the words of the Lord's Prayer rose to the windy sky. When it was over, Hamish picked up a spade and shovelled earth on to the grave. Mr Wellington spoke again. 'Mrs Wellington and I have a dram for all of you at the manse. All are welcome.'

The villagers began to file off. Hamish leaned on his spade and stared down at the grave. Off they all went down the hill in a silent procession. Some instinct told Maggie it would be the wrong thing to stay behind and so she went after them.

She turned back at the bottom of the hill. The tall figure of Hamish Macbeth was silhouetted against the windy sky. 'It's only a *dog*,' she told herself fiercely, but there was a sad dignity about the scene which caught at her throat.

Hamish stood there for a long time. Bright images of Towser chased each other across his brain: lazy Towser sleeping on the end of his bed; Towser giving Priscilla a rapturous welcome and putting muddy paws on her skirt; Towser running across the heather after rabbits. At last he gave a bleak little sigh, and with the spade over his shoulder, walked back down the hill.

The manse was full of people when Maggie arrived. She hesitated in the doorway of the living room. Mrs Wellington saw her and came forward. 'Come in, Miss Donald,' she boomed. 'A sad day, a sad day for all of us. Ah, here is Mrs Brodie, who is our doctor's wife. Mrs Brodie, this is a police constable, a Miss

Donald, who came with Hamish. Help yourself to a dram, Miss Donald.'

Maggie took a glass of neat whisky from a tray that one of the women was taking round the room.

'Is it this case over in Skag that you're on?' asked Angela Brodie.

'In a very minor way,' said Maggie. 'The detectives are the ones who are doing all the work.'

'Poor Hamish,' said Angela, pushing a wisp of hair out of her eyes. 'Murder seems to follow him around. But don't be misled by his lazy manner. He's very, very clever.'

'So I've heard,' said Maggie. 'What happened to his engagement?'

'You'll need to ask Hamish,' said Angela gently and Maggie felt snubbed.

She said quickly, 'I am surprised the whole village should turn out for the funeral of a dog.'

'We're a close-knit community,' said Angela. 'Towser meant a lot to Hamish. Here's Hamish now.'

Maggie could see Hamish's red hair above the crowd as he entered the room. There was a sudden silence and then they all crowded round him, soft Highland voices murmuring sympathy. Hamish took a glass of whisky and downed it in one gulp and then took another.

If he's going to get drunk, thought Maggie, I'll never get back tonight.

Angela introduced Maggie to one and then another. Soon the room was full of the sound of chattering voices. A man came in with an accordion and began to play jaunty reels. More whisky was passed round. The carpet was rolled back and some of them began to dance reels. Maggie, who had never been to a Highland wake before, was amazed at the noise and hilarity.

'They don't seem to be bothering much now about Hamish's dog,' she remarked to Angela.

'Oh, these things are a celebration of death. Everyone goes to heaven,' said Angela, 'even poor Towser.'

Hamish had joined in the dancing, his thin face alight, his long gangly limbs flying this way and that while they all cheered and clapped. More and more whisky, cigarette smoke, music and dance, people coming in from outlying villages bringing more bottles. By two in the morning, Maggie felt she had had enough. She had suggested twice to Hamish that they leave but he had ignored her.

'I'd better just go back to the police station and get to bed,' said Maggie to Mrs Wellington.

'That just won't do,' said the minister's wife. 'We'll find you somewhere. We have a spare bedroom. If you get your things from the station, we'll make you comfortable.'

'I didn't bring an overnight bag,' said Maggie. 'I did not expect to be staying.'

'Then come upstairs and I'll find you something.'

When Maggie was wrapped in one of Mrs Wellington's voluminous brushed nylon nighties, the minister's wife took away her clothes to wash. 'They'll be ready in the morning for you, Miss Donald. Sweet dreams.'

Maggie tossed and turned, trying to block out the noise from downstairs. Someone started playing the bagpipes. There was a noise as if someone had fallen over, and there was a crash of glass and then a noisy cheer. At last she fell into an uneasy sleep. She awoke early, feeling tired and jaded. To her surprise, her clean clothes were neatly laid on a chair at the end of the bed.

There was a wash-hand basin in the corner. Mrs Wellington had put out a new toothbrush still in its packet and a tube of toothpaste and clean towels. Maggie washed and dressed and made her way downstairs. The manse was silent. She decided to go to the police station and rouse Hamish.

She expected him to be passed out in a drunken stupor, but when she got there, she found Hamish in the kitchen with a middle-aged woman. 'I met you last night,' said the woman. 'I'm Miss Currie, Miss Nessie Currie.'

Hamish looked at Maggie. 'Could you give us a little time in private? I'll make you breakfast soon.'

Maggie nodded and went through to the living room. She waited and waited. She heard Nessie Currie leave and then, almost immediately afterwards, there was a knock at the door and someone else came in.

It was eleven o'clock in the morning when Hamish put his head around the door and said, 'Breakfast's ready.'

'More like brunch,' said Maggie. 'What was going on? Are people coming to report crimes?'

'No, they had some troubles they wanted help with.'

'So you're the local psychiatrist as well?'

'We all help each other.'

Maggie sat down at the kitchen table and tackled a substantial breakfast of bacon, eggs and grilled tomatoes. 'I think we'd better get back to Skag,' she said. 'I said we would be back last night, and this is not a day off.'

'I forgot,' said Hamish. 'Go through and phone Deacon.'

Maggie went through to the police office and closed the door behind her. She phoned the police station in Skag and asked for Deacon.

He listened while she told him about the funeral. 'These teuchters are all mad,' commented Deacon. 'Don't worry about it. Get back as soon as you can.'

Maggie went back to the kitchen and finished her breakfast. 'I hae a call to make before we leave,' said Hamish. 'We'll deal with it on the way.'

When they left the police station, he directed her to the seer's.

Angus Macdonald welcomed Hamish. 'Don't worry, Hamish,' he said. 'You'll get another dog.'

'I don't want another one,' said Hamish. 'This is Maggie Donald. You may ha' seen her at the manse last night.'

'Oh, aye.' The seer's eyes fastened on Maggie with an uncomfortably penetrating look. 'I'll put the kettle on.'

It's like the Dark Ages, thought Maggie, as the seer put a blackened kettle on a chain over the peat fire.

'I'll tell you why I've come to see you, Angus,' said Hamish severely. 'This nonsense has got to stop.'

'Whit nonsense?'

'And you call yourself a seer? I'm talking about Jessie Currie. Ever since you told her she would marry a divorced fisherman, she's evidently been going around painted up to the nines and behaving like a silly biddy. She hangs about the harbour when the fishing boats come in. Mrs Maclean's threatening to scratch her eyes out.'

'I see what I see,' said Angus portentously.

'You're a mischief-making auld scunner. Either you get Jessie up here and tell her you've had another vision, one that says she's going to lead a quiet spinster life, or I'll start to wreck your reputation and you know I can do it, Angus. A wee whisper in one ear, a wee lie in another.'

Angus looked at him thoughtfully. 'As a matter o' fact,' he said, 'I did have another sight o' her future.'

'I thought you might. Now I'm going to use your bathroom and then we'll be on our way.'

Hamish disappeared through the back of the cottage. 'So you won't be staying for tea?' the seer asked Maggie.

'No, we have to be going. We should have been back last night.'

'You'll be a successful young woman, that you will,' said Angus in a low crooning voice. 'You say you despise being treated as a sex object but you'll use that very sex to get to the top. You're a hard-bitten quean, young as you are.'

Maggie jumped to her feet, her face flaming. 'I'll wait in the car,' she snapped.

When Hamish came back, he looked around. 'Where's Maggie?'

'In the car.'

'Did you say something to her?'

'Och, no, the lassie wanted to be on her way.' The seer was confident that Maggie would not tell Hamish what he had said, and neither she did.

'Did you thank the Wellingtons for putting you up?' asked Hamish

'Oh, them; I didn't see anyone this morning, so I just left.'

Hamish gave a click of annoyance at the back of his throat. 'Go back to the village and stop at Patel's, the grocery shop.'

Maggie did as she was told. Hamish went into the shop and emerged carrying a box of chocolates. 'We'll call at the manse and you give that to Mrs Wellington and thank her for her hospitality.'

'How much?' mumbled Maggie. 'I'll pay you for them.'

'No need.'

Maggie was suddenly desperate to get out of Lochdubh. In the masculine world of the police force, she was used to men flirting with her, men making passes at her, but never men correcting her social manners.

Mrs Wellington thanked Hamish warmly for the chocolates. He said it was Maggie's idea. 'Oh, yes,' said Mrs Wellington. 'Thank you, Miss Donald.' Maggie had a sinking feeling that the minister's wife had already judged her as a hard, ungrateful piece of work who wouldn't dream of buying chocolates for her.

She drove out of Lochdubh with a feeling of relief. Never given much to introspection, she nonetheless felt she was leaving some rather nasty insights into her character behind.

It was with a feeling of relief that she dropped Hamish at the boarding-house.

She then drove straight to the police station. The station sergeant leered at her. 'Hey, Maggie, show us your knickers.'

'Cheeky sod,' retorted Maggie, batting her eyelashes at him, happy to be back in a safe, familiar world.

Deacon put his head round a door and saw her. 'Welcome back, Maggie,' he said. 'Bring us some tea and get some o' thae doughnuts frae the stores and we'll hear whit ye have to say.'

Maggie grinned. 'Right, boss.' As she turned to leave, she had the satisfaction of hearing Deacon say over his shoulder to someone in the room behind her, 'That's a grand lassie. She'll go far.'

Hamish went up to his room and sat on the bed and stared bleakly into space. Then he looked about. There was no sign of Towser's food or water-bowl or his leash. There was a soft knock at the door.

He rose wearily and opened it. Miss Gunnery stood there. 'I took the liberty of taking away Towser's things from your room, Hamish. I hope I did the right thing.'

'It wass verra kind and thoughtful of you, Miss Gunnery.'

'I'm sorry I was so cross about you going off with that policewoman. I'll take you into Skag for a drink, if you like.'

'Aye, that would be fine.'

When they were seated in the pub, Hamish asked, 'What's been happening?'

'Well, drama after drama. Dermott Brett's wife arrived. Did you know he and June weren't married? His name had been in the papers. There was such a scene. She said she was divorcing him. It turns out that the children are Dermott's. He was leading a double life for years, but he would never tell his wife because he said she couldn't live with it and she would do something mad like commit suicide, and the one good thing that's come out of it is that she actually wants rid of him, so he can marry June. He said, "Do you know, I never needed to have gone through all this?"'

Hamish's interest in the case was suddenly revived. 'I wonder what that could mean,' he said slowly. 'It could mean that he had no reason after all to kill Harris. What else?'

'Cheryl and Tracey were picked up this morning on the Dungarton Road trying to hitch a lift. The police have them along at the station.'

'Why were they running away?'

'Well, what I gather from that policeman, Crick, who's started gossiping because he's now bored with the whole thing, is that they were fed up with the dreadful food, the lack of talent and the police harassment.'

'Sounds reasonable. And what of Andrew and Doris?'

'It's so sad. They go for walks together, but they are so solemn. It's almost as if fear and worry are killing any love they might have had for each other.'

'And the children? What of the Brett children?'

'As soon as the wife appeared, June fortunately saw her coming and took the children out through the back door and kept them away all day. With any luck, June and Dermott can now get married after the divorce and the children need never know.'

'At least they're English,' said Hamish with feeling.

'What's that got to do with it?'

'If they were Scottish, under Scottish law they would stay bastards for the rest of their lives. Being English, they will be legitimized as soon as the parents are married. But how did Dermott manage to keep up the deception for so long?'

'Like Harris, he's a travelling salesman, mineral water. He's away a lot. He must work hard and earn a good lot of money to keep two households running.'

'Does he have any children by his marriage?'

'No, I gather not, from the informative Crick. And June changed her name to Brett by deed poll.'

Hamish's brain, which had been temporarily frozen by grief, suddenly seemed to be working again. That brothel! He had forgotten about that.

'I've a few calls to make,' he said. 'I'll see you later. I tell you what . . .' He thought of all Miss Gunnery's many kindnesses over the death of Towser. 'I'll take you out for dinner tonight. There's a good Indian restaurant in Dungarton. Do you like curry?'

Miss Gunnery's eyes shone. 'Love it.'

'Then that's a date.'

Hamish left her and walked along to the end of the main street to where he thought the house was that he had seen Harris leaving. It was a trim Victorian villa, set back a little from the road.

He went up and rang the bell. A plump woman, looking at first glance like any other Skag housewife, opened the door. She was wearing a summer dress and low-heeled shoes. Her brown hair was ferociously permed into hard curls and ridges. Her blue-grey eyes were hard and watchful and her mouth was small and thin, with a disappointed droop at the corners. She did not say anything, merely stood back to let him enter. She led the way into what in more respectable days would have been the front parlour. It looked a bit like a dentist's waiting-room. There were copies of glossy magazines on a low table in front of a sofa. A few occasional chairs stood about. A black marble clock ticked sonorously from the mantelpiece. Some dried pampas-grass in a bowl filled up the hearth. The room smelt of disinfectant and furniture polish.

'Well, whit can we dae for you?' she asked, folding her arms, her little eyes ranging up and down him.

'I am a police officer,' said Hamish, 'and I want to ask you a few questions.'

'Here, now, I have nae quarrel wi' the police at all.'

'I am not here to question you about running a brothel.'

An angry flush rose up her face. 'This is a respectable bed and breakfast, I'll have ye know. It's that Simpson creature you're wanting. I could hae you for slander. Off wi' ye.'

Feeling foolish, Hamish made for the door. 'Where does the Simpson woman live?'

'Next door.'

Muttering apologies, Hamish took his leave, sheepishly noticing as he reached the gate a little sign which advertised 'Bed & Breakfast' in curly script set by the gatepost.

The house next door did not look at all like a brothel from his limited experience. It had a trim, prosperous middle-class air. A new BMW was parked in the short gravelled drive at the side of the house.

He rang the bell, which played a cheerful rendition of 'Scotland the Brave'. This time the door was opened by a woman in a dressing-gown. She had a thin face, large teeth and prominent eyes. 'Oh, come ben,' she said cheerfully. 'You're early in the day.'

'It's the afternoon,' said Hamish.

'Aye, well, we're used to folk coming in the evening. What's your pleasure?'

She led the way into a front room. In contrast to next door, it looked more like a family living room. Someone had left some knitting abandoned on an armchair and the television was on. There was a small coal fire burning briskly in the grate. The sofa and chair were covered in flowered chintz.

'I am from the police,' said Hamish.

'Oh, aye, whit dae you want now? Another subscription to the Police Widows' and Orphans' Fund?'

Skating round this possible evidence of police corruption, Hamish said, 'I hope I haff the right place. Is this a brothel?'

'You're blunt.'

'I made the mistake of going next door first.'

She burst out laughing. 'That must ha' got the old biddy's knickers in a twist. I can tell you her gentlemen boarders, as she ca's them, drink mair than any o' the lot that come here. What dae ye want?'

'The man, Bob Harris, him that wass killed. Did he come here?'

'He came a couple o' times.'

'Who did he see?'

'Mandy, both times.'

'Can I speak to her?'

'Sure. But I doubt if she can tell you anything. It was a couple o' quickies, cheapest rate. I'll get her.'

Hamish waited. A low voice from the television informed him quietly of the mating habits of tigers.

After some time the door opened again and Mrs Simpson ushered in a pallid girl wrapped in a housecoat. Hamish did not belong to that sentimental class of men who consider that tarts have hearts. He had, during his police career, found them lazy, fidgety, nervous and cheeky.

'Here's Mandy,' said Mrs Simpson, pushing her forward. 'Don't take all day. She needs her beauty sleep.'

Mandy picked at a spot on the end of her long nose and then pushed her lank hair out of her eyes. Hamish reflected nastily that even if Mandy slept a hundred years, she would still wake up plain and grubby.

They sat down on the sofa. 'Now, Mandy,'

began Hamish, 'I believe the dead man, Bob Harris, was one of your clients.'

'Oh, him. I usually cannae tell one from the ither. But I saw his picture in the newspapers.'

'I feel if I knew a bit more about his character, then it might help me to find out who killed him.'

'Och, it waud be the wifie.'

'And what makes you say that?'

'He'd drunk a lot and he was suffering frae distiller's droop. Couldnae get it up. Said his wife had ruint him. Said she hated him. He said he'd be back but it was jist the same the next time. He smacked me around a bit, he was that mad. I rang the bell. We hae a bell in our rooms in case the clients get nasty and Mrs Simpson came running in and ordert him oot.'

'You must hear a lot of gossip from your clients. Has anyone mentioned seeing Bob Harris on the day he was murdered?'

'Aye.'

'What did he say? Who wass he?' Hamish leaned forward.

'It was that man from the boarding-house.'

'What? Next door?'

'Naw. The one where Harris was staying. Rogers. That's his name. Harry Rogers.'

Chapter Six

The whole world is in a state of chassis.
– Sean O'Casey

Hamish headed back along the beach in the direction of the boarding-house, loping his way through the long snakes of blowing white sand. He cut across the dunes towards the boarding-house and saw in the distance Rogers getting into his blue van. He ran even faster, shouting as he went, but the wind whipped his words away and he saw the van turn out on to the road towards Dungarton. Cursing because he hadn't a car and Miss Gunnery was probably still in Skag, he walked into the hall and found Maggie Donald standing there.

'Quick!' said Hamish. 'Have you got your car?'

'Yes, round the back, but –'

'Come on. We've got to get Rogers.'

They ran out and got into Maggie's car. 'Where to?' she asked.

'The road to Dungarton. He's driving his blue van.'

They sped off. 'What's it all about?' asked Maggie, swinging neatly round a tractor.

'I went to the brothel.'

'Why on earth . . .?'

'Rogers was a customer. And he said something to one of the girls about seeing Harris on the day he was murdered. Was there anything about that in his statement?'

'Not a word.'

'So let's catch Rogers and find out what he was doing.'

Maggie concentrated on her driving and they were rewarded on the outskirts of Dungarton by seeing the blue van in front of them. 'Should I flag him down?' asked Maggie.

'No,' said Hamish. 'I've a better idea. Follow him but don't let him see you. I want to see where he goes.'

Maggie let a car pass her so she was shielded from Rogers's view.

The blue van, travelling at a sedate pace, went through the centre of the town and then turned off into a leafy suburb on the far side where large Victorian villas stood on either side of the road. Once elegant private residences, they were now small hotels and retirement homes.

'He's stopping at that old folks' home,' said Maggie. Rogers had driven up the short drive of a villa which had a board outside it stating that it was the Sunny Times Retirement Home.

'Stop here,' ordered Hamish, 'and wait for me.'

Hamish slid out of the car. He went into the garden and peered round a laurel bush. Rogers was going to the kitchen door at the side of the villa.

As Hamish watched, a man in a greasy apron came out. Rogers handed him some notes. The man nodded and went back in. Rogers opened the back of the van. Soon the man appeared and together the pair began loading cartons into the back of the van.

Hamish strolled up. Rogers saw him coming. He slammed the back doors of the van shut and made quickly for the cab. 'No, you don't,' said Hamish. 'We'll chust be taking a wee look at whit's inside.'

'You need a search warrant,' shouted Rogers, his high colour even higher with rage.

'No, I don't,' said Hamish. He went to the back of the van and opened the doors and pulled one of the cartons forward. It contained a side of beef which smelt slightly high. He peered in the other boxes, which were full of assorted groceries. So this, then, was the reason for the horrible food at the boarding-house. Rogers was buying the rejects from an old folks' home in Dungarton.

Hamish shouted for Maggie and when she came up to him, he briefly outlined what he had found. 'Get that one out o' the kitchen,' he said, 'and we'll take them both in.'

Protesting loudly that it was all above-board and innocent, Rogers and the man from the kitchen were marched round and into the front door of the retirement home, where Hamish demanded to see whoever was in charge. A tired-looking man in a crumpled suit ushered them all into an office off the hall. He introduced himself as a Mr Dougald and said the home was run by a charity, Aid for the Senior Citizen.

'So what's Jamie been up to?' he asked wearily.

'Is this Jamie?' asked Hamish, nodding in the direction of the man from the kitchen.

'Aye, Jamie Sinclair.'

'He's been selling your stores to Mr Rogers here. Mr Rogers owns a boarding-house in Skag. He's been selling off meat which is well past its sell-by date. I hope it's old stores and you arenae giving the residents meat like that.'

'No, we are not. We get our supplies from reputable shops in Dungarton. This is what comes of employing ex-cons. I told the charity I didn't want Sinclair, but they said everyone needed a break.'

'What's Sinclair's form?'

'Fraud, petty larceny, shop-lifting, handbag snatching, you name it.'

Hamish settled down to question the now thoroughly cowed Sinclair. The housekeeper regularly checked the supplies in the fridges and freezers, and so the stuff he had collected for Rogers lay in a cupboard in the kitchen until the boarding-house owner came to collect it. Hamish charged Sinclair and Rogers with conspiracy to defraud the retirement home, told Maggie to take Sinclair out to the car, but curtly ordered Rogers to stay where he was. He turned to Mr Dougald. 'Can I use your office for a minute? I want to ask Mr Rogers a few questions before I take him to the station.'

'Go ahead. This is a bad business. But it'll teach all those do-gooders on the board to send me someone decent next time.'

When they had all gone out, Hamish faced a truculent Rogers. 'Now, the police at Skag will handle the charge, but I'm more interested in something else. You saw Harris on the day he was murdered.'

Rogers stared at him mulishly. 'I did not. Who says I did?'

'Some tart called Mandy at that brothel.'

Rogers, who had been standing, rocking on his heels, sat down suddenly, as if his legs had given way. 'No comment,' he mumbled.

'Och, well, maybe Mrs Rogers will have a few comments.'

'You wouldnae!'

'Try me.'

Rogers twisted his large beefy hands, one in the other, as if wringing an imaginary person's neck.

'All right,' he said after a silence. 'I saw him heading for the jetty. He was stopped by Dermott Brett, who was shouting at him. I couldnae hear the words.'

'When was this?'

'Around three.'

Hamish looked at him sharply. 'And why didn't Mr Brett tell the police this?'

Rogers stared at the ceiling. 'I don't know.'

'And why didn't you?'

Rogers stared at his feet.

'All right. Out to the car wi' you.'

Hamish left Maggie to explain the arrest of Sinclair and Rogers to Deacon. He borrowed Maggie's car and drove to the boarding-house. He wanted to question Dermott himself before the police came for him.

It was late afternoon but the wind had died and the sun was shining brightly. He saw ahead of him Dermott, June and the children on the beach. Dermott was helping the children build a sand castle and June was laughing at their efforts. They looked a carefree family party. He went up to them and said to

Dermott quietly, 'Walk away with me a little. I haff to talk to you afore the police arrive.'

Dermott put down the bucket-full of sand he had been holding and got slowly to his feet. He and Hamish walked away down the beach together beside the glittering waves of the incoming tide. Hamish glanced back. June was staring after them, her face pinched and anxious.

'I arrested Rogers,' began Hamish.

'Why?' A look of wild hope came into Dermott's eyes.

'Because of the rotten food. He'd been buying the leftovers from an old folks' home in Dungarton. But that's not why I want to talk to you. Rogers saw you arguing with Harris around the time of the murder.'

'Oh, that.'

'So out with it. Why didn't you say so in your statement?'

'I was worried. It would look bad for me. I panicked. I was trying to keep my name out of the papers. I thought if I told them, then a report would go out saying I was being detained to help the police with their inquiries and then my wife would have found out. As it was – you heard?' Hamish nodded. 'As it was, she found out anyway. She had always threatened to kill herself if I left her. And then she arrives, spitting venom. She'd read all about June and me being Mr and Mrs Brett in the papers, and she said she was going to divorce me. Just like that! All those years of covering up need never have happened!' He shook his head in bewilderment. 'I thought I was out of the wood. But . . .'

Hamish said quietly, 'But Rogers was blackmailing you.'

'Did he say so?'

Hamish shook his head. 'He was blackmailing you over having been in Skag, over having had a row with Harris before he was murdered.'

'He wasn't asking much,' mumbled Dermott, hanging his head. 'Just a couple of hundred. I thought I'd keep him quiet until this was over. Now it looks worse for me.'

'How did you pay Rogers?'

'I didn't. I was going to pay him today.'

Hamish groaned. 'I wish you'd given him a cheque. There'd be some proof then. It's his word against yours. Did you murder Harris?'

'I wanted to, but I didn't. He was hinting as how he'd let my wife know about me and June. I panicked. I followed him into Skag and threatened to punch him if he said anything. Rogers saw us. The minute he had the news of Harris's murder, he said he would tell the police I had been arguing with Harris. As I said, I panicked and promised to pay him.'

Hamish looked sadly across the beach. Two policemen were heading towards them.

'They've come for you,' he said. 'Take my advice and tell them everything. You've no proof o' blackmail, but now they know Rogers has been lying and cheating, they'll be inclined to believe you.'

Dermott walked off with the policemen. Hamish went up to June and, taking her a little away from the children, told her what had happened. 'We were mad to come back here,' said June bitterly. 'It was different last year. The food was good and the weather was perfect and the children loved it. What happens now?'

'Provided Dermott tells them the truth and they believe him, he'll probably be back this evening. But you must tell the truth as well, June. Where were you?'

'I was where I said I was, on the beach with the children. The only difference was Dermott wasn't here. He said he'd thought Harris had gone into Skag and he was going to shut his mouth.' High colour flared in her face. 'All he meant,' she added quickly, 'was that he was going to threaten to punch him.'

'Try to keep the children happy,' said Hamish. 'Little Heather's looking a bit strained.'

'She'll be all right,' said June. 'This is getting us all down. Who did it, Hamish?'

'I don't know.'

'Damn whoever it is to hell,' said June savagely. 'I hated Harris, but this murder is causing such worry and misery, I wish the man was still alive.'

'It's about tea-time. I wonder if there'll be any.' Hamish looked at his watch. June called the children. Hamish swung the youngest up on to his shoulders and together they all set off in the direction of the boarding-house, their shadows stretching out in front of them, long and pencil-thin. There was a faint hint of coldness in the air, reminding Hamish that any Scottish summer was of short duration and frost could set in before the end of August.

At the boarding-house, June took the children upstairs to change them.

Hamish went into the lounge. Miss Gunnery was sitting watching the news on television. She switched the set off. 'When are we going for dinner?'

Hamish had forgotten about his invitation to her but he rallied quickly. 'Oh, in about an hour. Have an early dinner. I feel tired.'

She stood up. 'In that case, I'll go upstairs and rest for a little before I change.'

Hamish walked to the window and looked out. He wanted to go to bed and sleep and forget about the whole thing. And yet he did not want to go up to his room, knowing that he would still expect Towser to run to meet him. The door opened and Doris and Andrew came in. They stopped short at the sight of him, looking wary. Then Andrew said, 'Are you coming into the dining room, Hamish?'

'No, I'm taking Miss Gunnery out. I don't know if there'll be any food tonight.' He told them about Rogers, ending up with, 'Dermott was a silly man to lie. It never does any good. While we're on the subject of lying, Doris, you said you walked away from the boarding-house in the opposite direction to Skag, but I myself saw you going in the direction of the village.'

'That's simple,' said Doris. 'I changed my mind and turned back, not along the beach but by the road, and then round the back of the house and down to the beach that way. Heather saw me.'

'Well, you'd better tell the police that. Where were you, Andrew?'

'I told you, Hamish. I went into Skag, hoping to find Doris, but didn't.'

Hamish looked at them uneasily. He was sure Doris had just told him an elaborate lie, and as for Andrew, he could easily have bumped into Harris. Skag was a small place.

'You know,' he said, rubbing his hands through his fiery hair in distress, 'I seem to keep saying this. It is no good lying to the police. They always find out one way or the other.'

'You mean even a fool like Deacon?' asked Andrew.

'Particularly a fool like Deacon. I have met the type many times. They are slow, tenacious and thorough. They can scent a lie, and when they are on the scent, they keep on questioning and questioning and digging and digging.'

'They can't keep us here forever,' whispered Doris.

'They can keep after you for the rest of your life. Whoever murdered your husband must be found, Doris. Don't you want to know?'

She flashed an odd little look at Andrew and said, 'I don't know.'

She thinks he did it, thought Hamish with a sinking heart. I'm sure of it. But if she thinks he did it, she can't have murdered her husband herself. Unless she's Andrew's Lady Macbeth and spurred him on to it.

It had been a long day. He felt suddenly weary. He nodded curtly to them and left abruptly and went up to change, reflecting as he rummaged for clean underwear that he would need to take a pile of dirty clothes to the laundromat in Skag, if it had one, the next day.

He put his head around the dining room door when he went downstairs again. June was serving up bacon and eggs to everyone. 'Mrs Rogers is at the police station,' she said.

'Bacon all right?' asked Hamish.

'Yes, I took it out of their own stores.'

He retreated. Miss Gunnery came down the stairs. She was very much made up and her hair was brushed down on her shoulders. She was wearing a print dress and white shoes. He had an uneasy feeling the spinster was falling for him and wished he had not invited her out for dinner. He ransacked his mind for an excuse but found none. And then the door opened and Maggie Donald walked in. 'You're to come to the station, Hamish. Deacon wants to see you.'

He felt relieved. Miss Gunnery looked bitterly disappointed and then she rallied. 'I'll wait for you, Hamish,' she said. 'You can't be all night.'

'Why don't we make it tomorrow night?' suggested Hamish. 'That'll be a firm date.'

'All right,' said Miss Gunnery reluctantly. 'I may as well get something in the dining room.'

'So what does Deacon want to see me about?' asked Hamish as Maggie drove him to Skag.

'I think he wants to talk to you about the case,' said Maggie. 'He wouldn't discuss it with a lowly WPC like me. And I thought you were taking me out for dinner tonight.'

'I forgot,' mumbled Hamish.

Maggie was feeling tired and her euphoria at being back among her 'own people' had quickly worn off. She had been excluded from all discussions of the case. Worse than that, she had tried to take full credit for the arrests of

Rogers and Sinclair, but Deacon had had an account from the two of how Hamish had caught them red-handed at the kitchen door and so had said, 'You'll get nowhere in the force, Maggie, if you're going to take credit for detective work done by someone else. I'm surprised at you. We could do wi' a cup o' tea. Hop to it.'

When they got to the police station, Maggie said, 'I'll wait for you in the car. If I go in there, they'll use me as a waitress, even though I'm off duty.'

Hamish went in and was directed into a side room by the desk sergeant.

Deacon was alone. 'Where are Rogers and Sinclair?' asked Hamish.

'Bound over to appear at the sheriff's court in Dungarton. That was a good bit o' work, Macbeth. Found out anything from thae folks at the boarding-house?'

But Hamish was too tired to 'betray' Doris and Andrew and voice his suspicions about them. He shook his head. 'Haven't had a chance.'

Deacon leaned back in his chair and pulled another one forward with his foot. 'Sit down, laddie. I've been thinking. Say it wasnae the wife or the lying Bretts or Rogers, or the wife's boyfriend. Have you thought o' your friend, Miss Gunnery?'

'Why her?'

Deacon tapped the side of his nose. 'Repressed spinster. All the guff about sleeping with you. I shouldnae believed it had she no' got herself up like a tart.'

'This is the nineties, not the nineteen hundreds,' said Hamish. 'Spinsters are often regarded as clever career women who've avoided the perils of marriage and children. They're not repressed or twisted, and as a matter of fact, statistics show that an unmarried woman is likely to have less illnesses and live longer. The only thing that might have sent them off their trolleys in the days before I wass born wass that society treated them as failures and freaks.'

'Oh well, have it your way,' said Deacon moodily. 'Did no one ever tell you in Strathbane to address your superiors as "sir"?'

'I forgot, *sir*; I happen to haff this mad idea that I am supposed to be on holiday.'

'Well, let's forget about the holiday that never was. Despite your appearance, you have the reputation of being a shrewd man. Now, say this case was on your manor, how would you go about it?'

'I would be among people I know well from the start. The Highlander is a different sort of animal.'

'Aye, ye can say that again. But I've been checking up on your cases. Some of the murderers were English.'

'Usually I would start by looking into the background of each suspect,' said Hamish. 'I know you've done that, but I have various connections outside the police force that I would use. There's only a pay phone in the boarding-house.' An idea struck him. 'I could maybe help you if you could give me a couple of days at my station.'

Deacon studied him for a moment and then said, 'Aye, I think we can let you go. We've no real reason tae keep ye. Take Maggie Donald wi' you.'

'Why?' demanded Hamish sharply. 'To keep tabs on me?'

'No, no,' said Deacon soothingly. 'We're giving you a helper, see? She's got good shorthand and typing. Can do any reports for you.'

Hamish did not want to take Maggie to Lochdubh, but, on the other hand, he was suddenly anxious to get away from Skag again. 'You'll need to let her pay for room and board if we stay overnight,' he said. 'Can't stay wi' me at the station.'

'Right. Where is she?'

'Out waiting in the car.'

'Off you go then, laddie, and keep in touch. Send Maggie in.'

Hamish went out to the car and told Maggie that Deacon wanted to see her.

Hoping that she was going to be given more important duties than tea-making, Maggie went eagerly in to see Deacon. When she heard she was to go with Hamish to Lochdubh 'and report back on everything he does', her face was almost comical in its dismay. 'Oh, not that hick place again,' she wailed. 'They're all weird. Do you know when Hamish buried his dog, the whole village turned up, just as if it were a real funeral, and they had a *wake*!'

'Aye, well, that's Highlanders for ye. Make sure you keep a close check on what he does and who he talks to. He's going back to use his own phone and get information from his own contacts.'

'What contacts can he have that we don't?'

'I don't know. All I know is that his methods, Watson, seem to hae worked for him in the past.'

When Maggie went back out to the car, Hamish said, 'Now, if you're to help me, do one thing for me.'

'What's that?'

'Go back in there and get the home addresses of all the suspects.'

'Easily done.'

Hamish sat and waited. He glanced at his watch. It hadn't taken long. He'd better get back and see if Miss Gunnery had eaten, and if not, take her out for dinner. As if his mind had conjured her up, a car drew alongside Maggie's and Miss Gunnery stepped out. Hamish got out as well.

'I came to see if you were all right,' said Miss Gunnery. 'I didn't want to find out you had been arrested again.'

Maggie came out. 'That's all set, Hamish,' she said. 'I've got the addresses you wanted. I'll pick you up at seven in the morning. Now what about that dinner you owe me?'

'I've a date wi' Miss Gunnery,' said Hamish. Both women stared at each other. I am a regular Don Juan, thought Hamish cynically. I get the pick o' the crop fighting ower me – one retired schoolteacher and one WPC so hard you could strike matches on her.

'Where are you going?' asked Maggie brightly.

'Hamish is taking me to some curry house in Dungarton,' said Miss Gunnery. 'He says it's good.'

'Oh, I can vouch for it,' said Maggie sweetly. 'I took him there myself.'

'Let's be off, then.' Hamish got into Miss Gunnery's car, fed up with both of them and with the whole of Skag and the murder case.

'Where are you off to tomorrow?' asked Miss Gunnery as they drove off.

'Back to Lochdubh. I have things to see to.'

'Are you coming back?'

'Of course. In a way, I suppose I'm still a suspect.'

'Nonsense.'

'I'd still have that in the back of my mind if I were Deacon. In a murder case, everyone is a suspect.'

'Even me.'

'Even you.'

'I loathed that man, Harris, and yes, I could have done it,' said Miss Gunnery, 'but I didn't. I would say good luck to whoever did, but the repercussions are so awful. Poor Doris. Why can't she go off with her Andrew and be happy?'

'I don't think either of them can be happy until the murderer is found. They may even suspect each other.'

'But that's ridiculous!'

'Not entirely. Don't you often look round at the rest of them and wonder which one of them it was?'

Miss Gunnery gave a little shiver. 'I keep hoping it will turn out to be some wandering maniac who just biffed Harris on the head to brighten up the day.'

'If it's a madman, then we're sunk. There's nothing worse than a motiveless crime.'

When they reached the restaurant and were seated, Hamish said, 'Can we talk about something else? I'm tired o' murder. Why did you retire so early? You don't look old enough to be at retirement age.'

'Flatterer. Near enough. I just got tired of school-teaching. I ended up teaching at a boys' school outside Cheltenham. I taught geography to a bunch of spoilt little brats who couldn't care less where anything in the world was situated. It's one of those public schools, not like Eton or Westminster or Winchester, but with very high fees. The boys who are sent there are usually ones who failed the Common Entrance exam, but their parents want them to go somewhere posh with expensive facilities. The pay was good, but training morons is always a strain. I thought of transferring to a girls' school and then decided to retire and enjoy myself.'

'And are you enjoying yourself?'

'I was, until this murder happened. It all seemed so gentle and safe, the idea of a cheap holiday in Scotland.'

'Back to the murder,' said Hamish ruefully.

'Then why don't you tell me some stories about your life, any that don't involve mayhem and murder.'

Hamish settled down to tell tales of Lochdubh, all his old affection for the place and the people coming back in force. How kind they had all been over Towser's death. He talked on and Miss Gunnery settled back to listen, her intelligent eyes twinkling with pleasure behind her glasses.

As they drove back to the boarding-house, Hamish realized with surprise that he had enjoyed his evening out with Miss Gunnery immensely.

But when the Victorian bulk of the boarding-house seemed to rear into view in the twilight, over sand dunes shaggy with spiked razor-grass, he felt his heart sink and wondered whether he should really be going away to Lochdubh, leaving a dangerous murderer on the loose in Skag.

Chapter Seven

I fled, and cried out, Death;
Hell trembled at the hideous name, and sigh'd
From all her caves, and back resounded, Death.
– John Milton

Lochdubh, again. Shafts of sun slanting down from the stormy heavens on the black waters of the loch. Fishing boats swinging at anchor. Clothes flapping and flying on clothes-lines like the loose sails of a distressed square-rigger.

Maggie, climbing out of the car at the police station, bent against the force of the warm Atlantic gale and followed Hamish into the kitchen. She had to sit and wait while Hamish lit the stove and checked on his livestock. He popped his head around the kitchen door and said, 'Why don't you run along to the manse and find out if you can get a bed in case we have to stay overnight?'

She hesitated. She was supposed to listen in to whoever it was he meant to phone. As if reading her thoughts, Hamish said amiably, 'I've got my chores to do. I won't be settling down to police work for about an hour.'

Maggie went off. Hamish grinned and went through to the police office. He took the list of names and addresses Maggie had given him. He phoned up his cousin, Rory Grant, a newspaper reporter in London, and after the pleasantries were over, he said, 'I'm in another murder case, Rory. The one in Skag. Heard about it?'

'Where the man got biffed on the head and pushed into the sea?'

'That one. Not the sea, though, the river. Anyway, if I give you the names and addresses of the suspects, can you see if there's anything on the files about them?'

'It's a dreary, parochial murder, Hamish. I mean, what's in it for me?'

'First crack at it if I find the murderer.'

'Not interested.'

'I was thinking of going down to Glasgow as part o' my research. Might call on your mother and tell her how you're getting on.'

'You wouldn't!' Rory knew Hamish was referring to his dissipated life of night-clubbing and womanizing.

'She'll be that anxious for news of you.'

'All right, you blackmailing pillock. Let's have them.'

Hamish read out the list of names and addresses. Having finished with Rory, he stared at the phone and at the addresses, phoned the police station in Cheltenham and asked them for the name of an expensive boys' school on the outskirts where the fees were high and the academic qualifications of its pupils low. They came up with the name and phone number of St Charles.

He telephoned the school and asked to speak to the headmaster, a Mr Partridge, who said testily he had already been interviewed by the police and had nothing more to add. Miss Gunnery had worked for them for several years as a quiet and efficient teacher. Her decision to take early retirement had certainly come as a surprise. Yes, she had lived in the school and had now, he believed, a flat in Montpelier Street.

That unsatisfactory call being over, Hamish then phoned a fourth cousin who worked at a garden centre in the Cotswolds and despatched him into Evesham to find out what he could about the Harrises. Hamish could have phoned the Evesham police, but Deacon would already have done that, and he knew his Highland relatives were better at digging up useful gossip than any policeman. The Bretts, or rather June and Dermott, lived in Hammersmith. With any luck, Rory might find something out about them. His pen hovered over the name of Dermott's real wife, Alice.

He sat back, his brow furrowed in thought. Now there was an unknown quantity. Would it be too far-fetched to assume that Harris had actually written to the wife, that she knew about her husband's double life before the murder? Had she come up before the murder, found Harris and knocked him on the head in a fit of rage? Married people could well turn savagely against the bearer of bad news. There was an address in Grays, Essex.

Rory had once introduced him to a newspaper stringer from Chelmsford in Essex. He fished in his desk and took out a large notebook. Hamish logged every name and address and phone number of anyone who might be useful that he met on his travels. Here it was. Harry Dixon. He phoned up and having got Dixon on the phone, outlined the case and asked if it would be possible to find out anything about the recent movements of Alice Brett. Dixon at first protested that he was getting old and didn't like working for nothing, and the inside story of a murder in the north of Scotland would hardly earn him anything. But Hamish said that he would see Rory's newspaper sent some work his way and so Dixon said he would do it.

Andrew Biggar had an address in Worcester. Hamish got out a road atlas and traced the road from Evesham to Worcester. Sixteen miles. Not far. Could Andrew and Doris possibly have met before? How irritating to be so far away. He telephoned the editor of a newspaper in Worcester and asked him to check up on the files and see if Andrew's name came up.

Tracey and Cheryl, he would leave to the police. Their criminal young lives were well-documented on police files and probation reports.

Maggie did not go to the manse. She decided she would rather pay for bed and breakfast than be beholden to the rather terrifying minister's wife. She saw a white board advertising bed and breakfast outside a cottage near the harbour and went and knocked at the door. It was opened by Mrs Maclean, Archie the fisherman's wife.

'Have you a room for a night?' asked Maggie. 'I'm –'

'I know fine who you are,' said Mrs Maclean. 'You're thon policewoman. I'm right glad to see Hamish is showing some sign o' decency at last. Come in. I'll show it to you.'

Maggie walked in through a kitchen filled with steam which came from a large copper pan full of boiling sheets on a stove in the corner. The air was full of the smell of bleach and washing soda. She was led upstairs and

Mrs Maclean pushed open a low bedroom door. Maggie was small for a policewoman, but she instinctively ducked her head as she entered the room. It contained a narrow bed with glittering white sheets and a fluffy white coverlet. There was a wash-hand basin and a basket chair and a narrow wardrobe.

'How much?' asked Maggie.

'Ten pounds.'

'Very well. I'll take it. Of course, we may finish our work today.'

Mrs Maclean folded her red arms across her pinafore. 'It must be a firm arrangement,' she said.

Maggie wanted to say she would look elsewhere, but had a feeling that in this close-knit village, word of her refusal to stay at Mrs Maclean's would spread like lightning and no one would want to put her up. And she was billing the police for her accommodation anyway.

'Very well,' she said, 'I'll go and get my overnight bag.'

'If ye have anything ye need washed, jist give it tae me. I aye wash the folks' clothes that stay here.'

The few clothes in Maggie's bag were clean but she was impressed by this offer of village laundry. It would be nice to have everything thoroughly cleaned and pressed. She had put in one pretty dress in the hope that she and

Hamish could go out for dinner somewhere. She was not particularly attracted to Hamish Macbeth, but he was a man and the only way she knew how to deal with the opposite sex was to try to get them sexually interested in her.

She got her bag from the car and returned to Mrs Maclean's with it and then returned to the police station. There was no sign of Hamish. She walked up the back of the police station and saw Hamish silhouetted against the windy sky. He was standing looking down on Towser's grave.

Maggie retreated back to the police station, feeling as if she had been conned. This was a useless journey. Deacon had overestimated Hamish's abilities. He was just one mad copper who had dragged her all the way here so that he could stand by his dog's graveside and mourn. She looked in the kitchen cupboards and the fridge. No food.

Then she remembered seeing an Italian restaurant as she had driven along the waterfront. She made her way there. It was quite full but a slim man with neat features showed her to a corner table and then spent an inordinate time washing and scrubbing the checked plastic tablecloth before handing her a menu. She ordered lasagna and a green salad and a glass of wine. To her surprise, the waiter stared down at her accusingly. 'You'll just be having the one glass of wine, I hope.'

'I'll drink a whole bottle if I feel like it,' retorted Maggie.

'My name is Willie Lamont.'

'So?' Another inbred local, thought Maggie.

'I was in the force myself afore I entered the restaurant trade,' said Willie severely, 'and there is one thing I cannae stand and that's a policeman who drinks, and a policewoman is even worse.'

Maggie bridled. 'One glass of wine is hardly over the limit. Now can you forget you ever were a policeman? Because I am hungry. Hop to it.'

Willie gave a last polish to the table and left. When Maggie's meal arrived, it was served not by Willie but a stunning-looking woman who could have doubled for Gina Lollobrigida in her hey-day. 'My husband has been telling me that you are with the force,' she said.

'Yes,' said Maggie curtly. Lucia, Willie's Italian wife, leaned a curved hip against the table. 'I am pregnant,' she said.

Maggie blinked. 'Congratulations.'

'I know it will be a boy,' said Lucia dreamily, 'and we will name it Hamish.'

'After Macbeth, I suppose?'

'Yes, it is a nice name . . . Hamish. So sad about his poor dog.'

'Very sad,' agreed Maggie, longing to be left

in peace to eat. She raised the glass of wine to her lips and lowered it when Lucia said severely, 'Willie tells me you drink a lot.'

Maggie put the glass down with a firm little click. 'Look here, I ordered one glass of wine. One! I am also very hungry. Do you mind leaving me alone to enjoy my meal?'

Lucia looked at her sadly. 'Poor Hamish,' she said. 'He never finds the right one. Me, I do not think that Priscilla was right for him, but she is kind, and you are not.' Lucia had a soft voice, but none the less it carried around the restaurant. The locals listened avidly. Lucia swayed off and Maggie bent her flaming face over her food. She ate and drank very quickly, calculated the price of the meal, left the money on the table and walked out, glad to escape from the hard stares of the other diners.

When she returned to the police station, she could hear the murmur of Hamish's voice from the office. She tried the handle of the door and found it was locked. Baffled, she retreated to the kitchen.

After some time Hamish emerged from the office. 'I thought I was to help you with this case,' said Maggie. 'Did you lock the door of your office so that I would not hear what you were doing?'

'Och, no,' said Hamish easily. 'I do it in case some of the locals chust walk in, which they have a habit of doing.'

'Have you found out anything?' asked Maggie.

'I've put in a few calls,' said Hamish. 'Now all I have to do is wait for the replies. There is one thing I did not ask Dermott.'

'Which is?'

'He told me that he did not know the boarding-house was under new management. There's something verra wrong there. I spoke to the surviving Miss Blane, one of the two that used to own the place. Now she told me that Dermott was well aware they were selling the place. That Dermott had had such an unpleasant experience with Harris the year before, and the Misses Blane had given him a lecture on "living in sin" with June. So why come back at all? Unless it was because he knew the boarding-house was under new management and it was cheap and that he did not expect to see Harris again. But what if he knew Harris was going to be there? I wonder if Dermott and Harris met at any time in the intervening year. They're both commercial travellers. There's another thing I've been wondering about. Tell me about Fred Allsopp.'

'The barman?'

'Aye, him. Harris was in the pub the day he was killed and getting drunk. Did he meet anyone, quarrel with anyone?'

Maggie shook her head. 'Fred said Harris was drinking whisky, quite a lot of whisky. He tried to get into conversation with some of the locals but they avoided him.'

Hamish shrugged impatiently. 'I have a feeling so many of the suspects are lying and probably for no reason at all. I haff found when the police are around that folks will lie almost automatically. Then there's something else. I wonder if Heather really saw Doris where she said she did, or if someone put her up to it, but that someone would be her mother or father, and why should they want to protect Doris?'

'Unless Dermott did it and didn't want Doris to be blamed,' said Maggie.

'The day I meet a kind and thoughtful murderer, I'll eat my hat,' said Hamish. 'Have you eaten?'

'I went to that Italian restaurant and got served by a cheeky sod called Willie Lamont who lectured me on the evils of drink.'

'Aye, that's Willie. He gets bossier and bossier and the portions are getting a bit small, but there's nowhere else to eat for miles unless it's the Tommel Castle Hotel, and that's pricey.'

'Does Willie own the place?'

'No, it's owned by a relative of Lucia's. He's been away in Italy. He'll be back soon, which means the food will be back to normal. I might be here until tomorrow. You'd best find a place to stay. Mrs Wellington would put you up.'

'I'm staying at a Mrs Maclean's.'

Hamish's eyes glinted with amusement. 'It's hygienic, I'll say that for it.'

The phone shrilled from the office and he went to answer it. It was from his relative in the Cotswolds. He said that he had checked on the Harrises in Evesham and had found pretty much what Hamish had expected – Doris was well liked and respected by the neighbours and Bob Harris had been detested by all. 'But,' added the soft Highland voice on the end of the line, 'a Mrs Innes who lives next door and who is friendly wi' Doris, well, herself said that Doris did not want to go back to Skag, she hadn't enjoyed it; but she said as how her man was up tae something.'

'Meaning Harris was up to something?' asked Hamish.

'Aye, chust so. This Doris had tried tae make a stand and say as how she wouldnae go back and Harris shouted at her and said he had his reasons.'

'Oho! Anything else?'

'That iss it so far. I'll keep in touch.'

Hamish thanked him and rang off.

As soon as he returned to the kitchen, Maggie asked him sharply who had been on the phone. Hamish felt a stab of irritation. This was a Watson he did not want.

Still, what was the harm in her knowing,

apart from the fact that he did not like her very much.

'That was a contact in Evesham,' he said. He told her what he had found out.

'This is interesting,' said Maggie. 'It looks as if Harris might have found out the Bretts were going and meant to be there to torment them.'

'If this was a detective story,' said Hamish gloomily, 'the least likely person would be the murderer, either Miss Gunnery or Andrew Biggar. But in real life it's always the obvious, and the obvious is either Doris or Dermott. Doris must have hated her husband, years of abuse building up in her, and Dermott admits he was terrified of his wife finding out. Ah, well, I'll need to wait in for any more calls. Why don't you take a walk around the village?'

'I am here on duty,' said Maggie, 'and I have seen all of this village that I want to see.'

'Suit yourself,' said Hamish. He went back into the office and firmly closed the door.

Maggie stifled a yawn of boredom.

The phone in the office rang again. She half got to her feet and then sat down angrily again. It was Hamish's job to tell her what he had found out.

Hamish picked up the phone and heard the cheery voice of Mr Johnson, the manager of the Tommel Castle Hotel. 'I heard you were back,' said Mr Johnson. 'How's things?'

'I'm working on this murder over at Skag,' said Hamish, 'but I'm here so that I can use my own phone. Heard from Priscilla?'

'Not for some time. She's still down south. At first she phoned almost every day, but, och, Hamish, there's nothing for her to worry about. Between you and me, it's easier to run the place without herself around. She worries so damn much. Coming up for a visit?'

'I can't. I'm waiting for people to return calls and I've got a WPC wi' me, checking on everything I do.'

'Bring her up for dinner tonight. I'll give you both a meal on the house. The colonel and missis are away, so I've got the run o' the place to myself. All the Halburton-Smythes are a pain in the neck, if you ask me.'

'Priscilla's all right,' said Hamish defensively.

'Oh, aye, but I sometimes think that lassie makes work. See you the night?'

'I'll bring my minder with me,' said Hamish. 'Can't verra well leave her behind.'

'Is she pretty?'

'So-so.'

'Give you a bit o' light relief.'

'Not this one. She's staying at Archie's.'

'My, my. She'll be scrubbed to death. Come around eight if you're free.'

Hamish was reluctant to return to Maggie. He had letters to write to various far-flung relatives and so he settled down to the task.

The day wore on. The phone stayed silent. Then, about four in the afternoon, it shrilled into life again. It was the stranger, Harry Dixon, from Essex.

'Alice Brett works as a legal secretary. I had to follow her up to Lincoln's Inn Fields. I'm billing you for the petrol. Before I went, I talked to the neighbours. Listen to this. A week before the murder, she got a letter and she told her friend and neighbour, Mrs Dibb, that she was going to Scotland because her husband had been cheating on her. I saw her in her office. She said Mrs Dibb was talking rubbish and that she received no letter and knew nothing about it until she saw Dermott's name in the papers. Went back to Mrs Dibb, who must have had a phone call from our Alice in the intervening time, for she shrieked at me that she had said nothing about any letter and slammed the door in my face.'

'Good work,' said Hamish. 'I'll get the police on to her.'

'I thought you were the police.'

'I am, I meant the southern police,' said Hamish, feeling caught out because he sometimes thought of the police as *them*, as if he himself were on the other side of the law.

Having a shrewd idea that if he told Maggie she might phone Deacon and claim the result as her own, he phoned Deacon himself and related what he had found out.

'I should be pleased wi' you,' said Deacon sourly, 'but all this means is yet another suspect. Anyway, you're doing fine. We'll get after Alice Brett.'

'This should work both ways,' said Hamish, 'Phone me with anything you've got on Alice Brett. And I'll be getting a petrol bill from my contact in Essex. I'll pass it on to you.'

'Right. Can I hae a word wi' Maggie?'

Hamish fetched her. In retaliation to Hamish's behaviour, Maggie shut the door of the office on *him*.

She was annoyed to find out that there was nothing new she could tell Deacon, Hamish having told him more than she knew. 'Can't see much point in me being in this dead-alive place,' said Maggie.

'You just help Macbeth,' said Deacon sharply. 'That's what you're there for.'

The phone rang almost as soon as she had put it down. She picked it up quickly. 'Hamish?' demanded a voice. Maggie was just beginning to say, 'This is WPC Donald. I will take any messages for PC Macbeth', when Hamish strode in and snatched the phone from her. 'Hello, Rory,' she heard him say. Maggie sat down in a chair in the office, determined to hear this call. What Rory was actually reporting was that he had found nothing on the files about any of the suspects, but all Maggie could hear from her end was Hamish's grunts of disappointment. Hamish replaced the receiver and said to Maggie, 'What about a cup of coffee?'

'You're as bad as the rest of them,' said Maggie, slamming out.

The phone rang again. It was the editor of the newspaper in Worcester. He said he had found a few cuttings on Andrew Biggar; he had judged a dog show last year, ridden in one of the local point-to-points, lived with his mother in a large house outside Worcester on the Wyre Piddle road; nothing else.

Hamish thanked him, rang off and stared in frustration at the phone.

He went back into the kitchen. Maggie was looking depressed. 'Forget the coffee,' he said abruptly. 'We'll go and call on Angela, the doctor's wife, instead. Get you out a bit. And I'm taking you for dinner to the Tommel Castle Hotel tonight.'

Her face lit up. 'Oh, Hamish, how kind! That will cost you a lot.'

'Don't worry about it,' he said grandly, having no intention of telling her that the meal was to be free.

Feeling suddenly pleased with him, Maggie followed him out and they walked towards the doctor's house, leaning against the screaming wind. Waves curled and smashed down on the pebbles of the beach. A plastic dustbin rolled crazily past them. Children ran before the wind on the beach, screaming like seagulls. Hamish and Maggie walked round the side of the doctor's house and Hamish knocked at the kitchen door.

Angela answered it and invited them in. Maggie looked curiously around the kitchen. Books everywhere: on the kitchen table, on the chairs and on the floor. Two cats promenaded lazily across the books on the table and two dogs snored under it.

'Clear a space for yourselves, Hamish,' said Angela. 'You know the drill in this house.'

While she prepared a jug of coffee, Angela said over one thin shoulder, 'So how's the case going, Hamish, and why here and not in Skag?'

'I wanted the use of my own office,' said Hamish. 'How's life in the village?'

'Much the same. No dramas. Jessie Currie has gone back to being an ordinary lady. Whatever Angus told her seemed to do the trick, although she looked quite sad for a few days. There's a cake sale up at the church hall tomorrow and I tried my best, but my cakes never rise. We've had various visitors looking at the Lochdubh Hotel.' She turned round and said to Maggie, 'It's been up for sale for some time. But they always go away again. There was even a consortium of Japanese business men, but the minute they saw the hills and mountains and found there was no way of attaching a golf course to it, they left again.

Oh, yes, there was a drama last week. Didn't you hear about it at the manse?' Hamish shook his head. 'There were plans to make it into a sort of approved school for young offenders. I think everyone in the village wrote to their MP to protest.'

'It is a fine building and right on the harbour,' said Hamish. 'You would think someone would want it.'

'If the Tommel Castle Hotel had not come into being, then someone might have bought it, but no one wants to start up in an area where there's such a powerful rival.'

'Any sign of the colonel turning it back into his family home?' asked Hamish. 'He must be as rich as anything now.'

'He got such a fright when he went broke last time,' said Angela, setting a jug of coffee on top of a pile of books on the table. 'He won't contemplate it. Johnson's a good manager.' She poured two mugs of coffee. 'Heard from Priscilla?' asked Angela.

'No,' said Hamish curtly, his face set.

'Oh, well,' said Angela quickly, 'tell me about this case.'

Maggie listened carefully as Hamish succinctly outlined the facts of the murder case and described the suspects.

Angela sat down with them as Hamish talked. 'Well,' she said when he had finished, 'you'll probably find it's this Dermott Brett.'

Hamish thought of Dermott and June and the children. 'I don't want it to be,' he commented. 'What about Dermott's wife, Alice?'

Angela frowned and pushed a wisp of hair out of her eyes. 'I'd like to know a bit more about her,' she said. 'I mean, a legal secretary doesn't actually sound like the hysterical type, but this Dermott obviously loves his June and yet was frightened to ask for a divorce in case his wife topped herself.'

'I wish I could be in about five places at once,' said Hamish. 'This business of Andrew Biggar and Doris bothers me. Evesham and Worcester are not that far apart. Do you believe in love at first sight, Maggie?'

Maggie, having never been in love, shook her head.

'And yet I sometimes think there was something between them afore they met up. Andrew Biggar lives in a big house outside Worcester, he apparently leads the life of a gentleman, and yet he comes to a low-class boarding-house in an inferior Scottish resort for a holiday. Damn. I'd like to get down there and question people.'

'Or it could be Miss Gunnery,' said Angela. Hamish looked at her in surprise. 'Why?'

'By saying she had slept with you, she gave herself a cast-iron alibi and she does not sound like a stupid woman.'

'But there's nothing about her to suggest the murderess,' said Hamish, exasperated. 'A blameless schoolteacher who appears to have led a blameless life.'

Angela sighed. 'None of us has led a blameless life, Hamish. We all have some sort of skeleton in the closet. But then you might find out it's this Cheryl and Tracey; have you thought of that?'

'I haven't really considered them. Their nasty young lives are so well documented, what with prison records and probation records.'

'But,' said Angela eagerly, 'that's just it. You've been concentrating on a lot of respectable people trying to find a murderer. But here you have two young girls with criminal records and one of them has been found guilty of violence. You say they were overheard saying they would like to kill someone for kicks. It might be as simple as that. You are looking for someone with the sort of character that would kill. Cheryl and Tracey fit the bill.'

'They're awfy young,' said Hamish.

'But very young children commit dreadful murders these days,' put in Maggie, who was beginning to feel she had been forgotten.

'I'll check up on them myself,' said Hamish. 'I hae a lot o' contacts in Glasgow.'

'The way I see it,' said Angela dreamily, 'is that it was a murder of savage impulse, no poisoning or shooting or stabbing, just a sudden blow to the head. Whoever it was may not even have contemplated murder. Just bashed the horrible Harris on the head in a fit of rage. Harris tips over into the river and the assailant rushes off without waiting to see the result of the blow. It was death by drowning, wasn't it?'

'Yes,' said Hamish slowly.

'So we get back to the respectable section of the boarding-house party,' said Angela eagerly. 'Instead of looking for a murderer, look for someone who might just be capable of a fit of rage. Oh, and there's something else.'

Maggie looked at the doctor's wife in irritation. It should have been she, Maggie, who should have been enthralling Hamish Macbeth with her speculations.

'What else?' asked Hamish.

'Harris seemed to like having things on people, like tormenting Dermott. And what if Harris knew about the bad food from the old folks' home? What of that? This Rogers. Now there's a criminal for you.'

'Aye, you've given me a lot to think about,' said Hamish. 'That business about Rogers now, I think Deacon should get on to it.'

Maggie got to her feet. 'Don't worry. I'll phone him, Hamish.'

'Oh, there's no need to go back to the police station,' said Angela to Maggie's fury. 'Use the phone over there, Hamish.'

So Maggie had to sit, feeling useless, as Hamish outlined his suspicions about Rogers to Deacon. The fact that she herself had not really had one good insight into the case did not occur to her. She felt she was being left out as usual.

When Hamish returned, he looked shrewdly at Maggie's sulky face and said, 'Why don't you run along and get changed for dinner and make your own way up to the hotel. I've a few calls to make.'

Maggie did not want to go, but on the other hand could think of no reason for staying, but as she walked along to Mrs Maclean's she was cheered by the fact that Hamish Macbeth thought enough of her to buy her an expensive dinner.

She sat in her room and read, occasionally glancing with pleasure at her newly laundered clothes, which had been laid out on the bed. The cotton dress she planned to wear was white, with great splashes of red roses. She knew it flattered her figure. Finally she went to the Macleans' minuscule bathroom and had a bath in one of those modern plastic baths which had about as much space as a coffin.

It was when she started to put her clean clothes on that she realized the sheer folly of having agreed to Mrs Maclean's laundering her clothes. Mrs Maclean must have boiled everything. The dress was cotton, the bra and panties of a cotton-and-acrylic mixture, as were the petticoat and tights. Everything had shrunk. The dress was up above her knees and strained painfully across her bosom. Her bra and panties felt tight and uncomfortable. She glanced at the clock. It would have to do. But she would give Mrs Maclean a piece of her mind on her way out.

But when she went into the kitchen, Mrs Maclean turned round from the steaming copper. Her face was flushed and red and her eyes very hard. Maggie's courage ran out. She simply walked past her and out of the door.

There had been no mirror in either Maggie's room or in the bathroom – how the husband shaved, she didn't know – and she had made up her face using the hand mirror in her compact.

As soon as she walked into the reception area of the hotel, she was faced by a reflection of herself in a long mirror on the opposite wall. She wanted to turn and run. Her large breasts, cut by the brassiere underneath and constrained by the shrunken dress, bulged over the low neckline like those of an eighteenth-century tart.

And then Hamish approached her, Hamish in a dinner jacket, looking very smooth and relaxed. 'I see you let Mrs Maclean wash your clothes,' he said sympathetically. 'Mistake. You can't eat in that dress. The food'll stick in your neck. Go and sit in the bar and I'll see what I can do.'

Maggie went and took a seat in the corner of the bar. As she walked across it, a group of men with gin-and-sauna-flushed faces watched her with amusement. One said with disastrous clarity, 'Must be the local tart.'

She sat there feeling naked and very alone. Hamish reappeared with Mr Johnson in tow. 'My, my,' said Mr Johnson, staring at Maggie in admiration. 'When Mrs Maclean washes, she really washes.'

'Come with me, Maggie,' said Hamish. 'I've got something for ye.'

He led her upstairs and along a corridor and took a key out of his pocket and opened the door. 'This is Mrs Halburton-Smythe's quarters. We'll find you something here, but don't spill anything on what you wear, or we'll all be in trouble. Here, what about this thing?'

He took out a caftan, a purple silk one embroidered with gold.

'Oh, that'll do,' said Maggie, looking at the gown's generous folds.

'The bathroom's through there,' said Hamish, 'I'll wait for you.'

Maggie, in the bathroom, removed the hellishly tight dress and underwear and slipped the loose caftan over her naked body. She left her discarded clothes in the bathroom so that she could change back into them when the evening was over.

When she came out, she asked, 'Is there a stole or a wrap or anything to put over this?'

'Bound to be,' said Hamish, searching through female garments. 'Oh, here's the very thing.' He handed her a black cashmere shawl, which Maggie gratefully put around her shoulders.

As they walked downstairs together to the dining room, Maggie stole sharp little glances at her companion. He seemed transformed by the dinner jacket. He looked as if he had been dining in expensive restaurants all his life. Maggie did not know that Hamish was blessed with the Highlander's vanity of feeling that he belonged anywhere he happened to be and so always fitted in.

Although Maggie enjoyed her dinner, she could not find any ideas to top those of the doctor's wife. Hamish did not exactly discuss the case with her, he seemed to be thinking aloud, almost forgetting she was there. In fact, thought Maggie, he did not seem to be aware she was a woman at all. Fortunately for Hamish, her self-consciousness stopped her from noticing that the waiter did not present him with any bill at the end of the meal.

When she had finally changed back into those dreadfully tight clothes, she felt quite demoralized. She knew she would not even have the courage to give Mrs Maclean a lecture. The rest of her small stock of clothes was probably just as tight. She would need to wash what she had taken off that day in the hand basin in her room and dry everything in front of the room's two-bar electric heater.

They were just leaving the hotel when Mr Johnson came running after them.

'Call for you, Hamish,' he shouted. 'The police at Skag.'

Maggie waited in her car. Hamish seemed to be away a long time. As he came out, she wound down her window. 'Trouble?' she asked.

'Aye. You'd best get down to Mrs Maclean's and pack up your things. We're off to Skag.'

'What's happened?'

'Another murder.'

'What! Who?'

'Thon Jamie MacPherson, the boatman.'

Chapter Eight

We must never assume that which is incapable of proof.

– George Henry Lewis

Smells of fish and chips and salt sea, cold wind, blowing sand, bleakness; only the end of July, and yet a strong suggestion of a dying year. Skag.

It was two in the morning. Hamish sat in the police station facing an unshaven Deacon.

'Tell me again, sir,' said Hamish. 'How did it happen?'

'If I knew how, I would know who,' said Deacon crossly. 'But as I said, it was like this: Mrs Flaherty and her husband wanted to take a boat out. It was late afternoon. They go to the boat-shed, that shack, you know, at the back o' the jetty. They go inside and look about. No one seems tae be there. Then, like a Hitchcock movie, missis sees a foot stickin' out from the back o' the door to that wee office he has at the back where he keeps his records. Well, they don't think o' murder, do they? Think some poor sod has passed out. Mr Flaherty says he's probably drunk but they have a look anyway. Jamie MacPherson is very dead. Mr Flaherty prides himself on his cool nerve and promptly tries to give mouth-to-mouth resuscitation. To do so, he slides one hand under Jamie's neck. That's when he feels wet stickiness, pulls his hand away and finds it covered wi' blood. Shows his hand tae his wife, who starts screaming like a banshee. So the first estimate by the pathologist and by the forensic boys is that Jamie was sitting at his desk when someone stabbed him in the back of the neck wi' something like a dagger, but not all that sharp.'

'So it would take some muscle to stab him?'

'Aye, that's the way it looks. He fell off the chair, backwards, knocking the chair over, rolled towards the door, and died on his back behind it. So either this is not related, or Jamie knew something and was blackmailing someone and that someone did for him.'

'And we haff the blackmailer in the shape of Rogers.'

'Aye, but at roughly the time o' the murder, Rogers was here, being questioned again. In fact, he was here all afternoon.'

'What about the rest of them?'

'Dermott Brett was interviewed again at lunch-time and sent away, Doris Harris and

Andrew Biggar were interviewed again in the morning, as was that Miss Gunnery. Cheryl and Tracey say they were on the beach, but nobody saw them.'

'If Jamie MacPherson was trying to make money out of someone,' said Hamish, 'then someone's bank account is going to show a recent withdrawal that someone might not be able to explain.'

'We're working on that.' Deacon passed a weary hand over his face. 'Do you know, I've got a gut feeling someone murdered Jamie MacPherson, *if* he was a blackmailer, before the first payment was made. I don't know what the weapon was.'

'Would it haff been something that wass just lying around?' suggested Hamish. 'A paper-knife, boat-knife, something like that?'

'Aye, it could well be.'

'What about family? Was he married?'

'Wife died a whiles back. One son in America. That's all. He lived alone, the auld bugger, so there's no one that we know of that he might hae confided in. Solitary bloke. No friends. Bit o' a quiet drunk, from all reports, solitary drunk.'

'I hate being stuck here,' said Hamish after a short silence.

'Why? This is where it's all happening, laddie.'

'There's something nagging at me. Doris Harris lives in Evesham and Andrew Biggar in

Worcester. They weren't far from each other. The horrible Bob was a traveller, so Doris must have had some time to herself. Now Andrew Biggar appears to be the country gent, large house with mother outside Worcester, judges dog shows, rides in local point-to-points. If he even keeps one horse, that's an expense. Someone like that does not suddenly decide to holiday in a tatty cheap boarding-house on the Moray Firth.'

'Okay,' said Deacon. 'Let's look at it. The gentlemanly Andrew is madly in love with Doris. So why the hell would he want to torture hisself by seeing her in company wi' her dreadful husband, eh?'

'Unless,' said Hamish quietly, 'he planned to murder Harris afore he came. Now you can get the local police at Worcester to dig deep, if you like. But you know what police routine is like. One bored constable or detective constable sent to ask patient questions. But I hae the knack of finding out things,' said Hamish with simple Highland vanity. 'I would like fine to get down there and see what I could come up with.'

'And what could you do that any detective could not?'

'Use my imagination,' said Hamish eagerly. 'Figure out if I were Andrew and meeting Doris on the sly, a Doris who would be terrified of any neighbour seeing her. I could figure out where they would meet. They don't look like a couple who've slept together, so I would be asking at the sort of restaurants or pubs they would go to, that sort of thing.'

Deacon leaned back in his chair and surveyed Hamish's tall figure. 'How do I cover for ye? You'd need to do it at your own expense and without the local police knowing.'

'I'll take a gamble,' said Hamish. 'If I solve this case, I'll leave it to you to fiddle the books to cover my costs. If not, I'll pay for it. I brought the police Land Rover wi' me. I could use that to get me south and then hire a car in Worcester or use public transport. I've done this sort o' thing before.'

'With results?'

'Always with results,' said Hamish, firmly tucking away in the back of his mind several wasted trips south.

'All right,' said Deacon suddenly. 'I'll do it. We'll say some relative of yours in the south has died. This is just between you and me. But don't be long. Two days at the most. I've photos of Doris and Andrew taken by the local man I can give you.'

Hamish drove back to the boarding-house in the Land Rover, which still smelt disturbingly of dog. He entered the unlit hall and stiffened as a dark shape on the staircase rose in front of him.

'Hamish?' came Miss Gunnery's voice.

'What are you doing there?' he demanded.

'I couldn't sleep. I heard from that policewoman that you'd returned. You've heard about this other murder?'

'Come into the lounge,' said Hamish.

He switched on the lights and they sat down facing each other. She was still dressed. Black shadows circled her eyes. She seemed all at once old.

'I'm going away tomorrow,' said Hamish.

'Oh, no. You mustn't. I'm frightened.'

'I'll be gone two days at the most,' said Hamish soothingly. 'I'm going to Evesham and Worcester. What are the others saying about this latest murder?'

'Dermott and June are protecting the children as much as possible, so they're very quiet. The noisiest was Cheryl, who went into hysterics, screaming she knew she would be next. Mrs Rogers has gone to stay with a relative in Dungarton, so we have to cook our own food, not that that's a hardship. I was thinking of leaving and then this other murder happened, so we're all trapped in this dreadful place.'

'I won't be away long,' Hamish explained again.

'I don't know why they are keeping us,' said Miss Gunnery, a nervous tic jumping on her left cheek. 'What can the murder of that boatman have to do with Harris?'

'Jamie could have been blackmailing the murderer,' said Hamish flatly.

'But that's ridiculous!'

'Maybe. But it's a strong possibility. He was an odd, solitary man and a drunk. Go to bed, Miss Gunnery. I need a few hours' sleep. I've got an early start.'

'Could you do something for me?'

'Depends what it is,' said Hamish cautiously.

'You won't be far from Cheltenham. Could you possibly call on Ada, my friend Ada Agnew? Tell her I'm all right.'

'You could phone her.'

'I know. It's silly of me. But Ada is looking after my cat and I'm sentimental about that animal. He's called Joey. Just call and see if the cat looks all right. Dear me, I sound like an old maid.'

'Give me her address and I'll call if I can,' said Hamish.

Miss Gunnery stood up and took an old magazine and tore off a strip of the margin and wrote 'Mrs Agnew, 42, Andover Terrace, Cheltenham' on it and passed it to Hamish.

He suddenly felt exhausted. He gave her an abrupt 'Goodnight' and strode out without waiting to see whether she followed him or not.

Hamish had told Deacon that he would leave at seven in the morning but he actually left at six, frightened that he might find Maggie Donald waiting for him on the doorstep at seven.

It was with a feeling of relief that he drove off from Skag and took the long road south. The motorways farther south made it a relatively easy journey and it was late afternoon when he arrived in Worcester, finding a bed-and-breakfast place on the London road. Although he was tired after his long drive, he washed and changed and phoned around for the cheapest car-rental place he could find, eventually settling for a doubtful firm called Rent-A-Banger. The couple who ran the bed and breakfast were elderly and with a refreshing lack of curiosity as to why a Scottish policeman would wish to leave his Land Rover in the street at the back of their house while he rented a car. The house was dark and old-fashioned, but his room was comfortable.

He picked up an old Ford Escort from the rental firm and headed out on the Wyre Piddle Road towards Andrew's home. It was only when he was on his way there that he began to feel rather silly. All around Worcester there were pubs and restaurants, not to mention all those in the town itself. This was not the far north of Scotland. There were hundreds of places where a couple could meet. Andrew's home was called High Farm. As he approached, he saw that it had indeed been at one time a farmhouse but was now a private dwelling, the outbuildings converted to stables and garages. He could see it all clearly from the road. He pulled into the side and wondered what to do. It was then he saw a tall, powerful-looking woman with white hair emerge and get into a Range Rover and drive off. There was something about her features that made him sure that this must be Andrew's mother. After she had gone, he continued to study the house. He noticed a burglar alarm box on the wall of it and wondered whether the place was really wired up or if it was just an empty box to deceive burglars. It was in that moment that he realized that all the while he had subconsciously been planning to break in. Ignoring the warning voices in his head, which were screaming at him that it would mean the end of his lowly career as constable of Lochdubh if he were caught, he drove a little along the road until he came to a side road. He drove up it, parked the Ford close in under an overhanging hedge, and then strolled back. There was no one around. The house was large. They might have a servant who lived in. But the place had the deserted blind air of a house when no one is at home. To be on the safe side, he rang the bell and waited. There was no reply. Looking all about him to make sure no one was watching, he ambled around to the back of the house, which was two-storeyed and of red brick.

There was a one-storey extension on part of the back of the house. He peered in the window. It was an extension to the kitchen area. He backed off and looked up and then a smile curved his lips. For above the flat roof of the extension was an open window with two cats lying on the sill. He thought briefly of Miss Gunnery and sent up a silent prayer of thanks to all cat lovers. Still, he had better move fast. The very fact that she had left a window open for the cats meant she did not mean to be away long.

He climbed nimbly up the drain-pipe on to the flat roof and gently shooing the cats inside, quietly raised the window and eased himself in over the sill.

He found himself in an upstairs corridor. He opened one door. Box-room. He shut it and tried the next. This was obviously Andrew's bedroom: photographs of army groups on the walls, older photographs of university days, Rugby-team photographs. But Hamish was looking for letters.

There was a desk by the window. He carefully sifted through tax accounts and various bills, replacing every bit of paper exactly as he had found it. Night was falling. It would soon be dark here compared to the north, where it would still be light. He quickened his search, not wanting to be forced to switch on a light.

He let out a click of exasperation. There were no private letters at all, only business letters. There were no photographs apart from the ones on the walls. He turned away from the desk to a low bookshelf and carefully took out book after book and shook it, hoping that

Andrew had hidden a photograph or letter in one of them, but there was nothing except the occasional bookmark.

Perhaps he had a study downstairs, thought Hamish, another desk where he kept more personal things. He made his way quietly downstairs. He opened the door of a small but pleasant sitting room. Here were family photographs in silver frames. There were various groups. Andrew at school, Andrew at university, Andrew at Sandhurst, and so on.

And then he heard a car driving up. He made a dash for the door, tripped over a cushion which he hadn't seen lying on the floor, and measured his length on the carpet. He scrambled on his hands and knees behind the sofa, cursing silently. Mrs Biggar, Andrew's mother, for it must surely be she, obviously moved very quickly, for she was inside the house and inside the sitting room only moments after Hamish had heard the car arrive. He lay behind the sofa, and sweated. He heard her cross to the fireplace. The fire must have been already made up, for soon after the striking of a match, he heard the crackle of burning wood. He hoped she would leave the room, but the sofa creaked as she sat down on the end of it.

And then the telephone in the room rang loudly, making him start.

He heard her answer it, heard her say sharply, 'Andrew?'

There was a silence. Hamish desperately wished he could hear what was being said at Andrew's end of the line.

Then Mrs Biggar said, 'Another murder! Andrew, this is dreadful, dreadful. But don't say I didn't warn you.'

Another silence, then Mrs Biggar said, 'I wish to God you had never become involved with that woman.'

A faint noise came from the other end of the line, Andrew protesting or explaining.

'You should have told the police,' complained Mrs Biggar. 'What if anyone saw the pair of you? No, don't tell me about discretion . . .

'Where? Well, that old cat Harriet Gourlay saw you in that Chinese restaurant in Evesham for a start. It's all most unlike you. And now you see what comes of knowing those sort of people. They're always beating each other up or murdering each other.'

Another long silence. She said in a softer voice. 'I know you don't want me to come up, but if you need a lawyer or anything, you must let me know . . .

'Right, phone me at this time tomorrow if you can. Goodbye, darling.'

The receiver was replaced.

Go away, prayed Hamish silently. Oh, please, go away!

He heard her moving about the room and pressed his thin body even closer to the back of the sofa. And then one of the cats strolled round the back of the sofa. It climbed on to his chest and began kneading its claws into his sweater.

He glared at the cat, willing it to go away, but with the cat's genius for loving where it is not wanted, it transferred its affections to his chin by butting its furry head against it. Its fur tickled Hamish's nose. He felt a sneeze coming and twisted his body round to dislodge the cat. To his relief he heard Mrs Biggar leave the room. He took a swipe at the cat and missed. It pranced away happily. He heard a faint clatter of dishes in the distance. He eased himself to his feet. He went through the open door of the sitting room and into the hall. To his immeasurable delight, the door stood open. He slipped outside. Then he stopped. He could not risk her seeing him walking away from the house. He turned about and rang the bell.

She came to the door, wiping her hands on an apron. 'Yes?'

Hamish fixed her with a steely glare. 'Have you found God?'

'Go away!' she said and slammed the door in his face.

He walked off down the drive, feeling almost light-hearted at having got clear away.

He found his car where he had left it, got in and headed for Evesham. It had been scary, but overhearing that phone call had been marvellous. He could not tell Deacon that he had broken into Andrew's house and that was how he knew the couple had met before. But if he took those photographs of Andrew and Doris to the right Chinese restaurant and the owner recognized them, then that would be proof enough.

Once he reached Evesham, he parked the car and decided to search on foot, knowing that country towns can have bewildering one-way traffic systems. A couple directed him to a Chinese restaurant in the High Street, saying that the other Chinese places, as far as they knew, were mostly take-away shops. It was housed in an elegant wood-panelled Carolean building. He asked the waiter for the manager or owner and a sober-suited Englishman appeared from the back premises. Hamish explained who he was and where he was from and produced the photographs of Doris and Andrew and then waited hopefully.

To his disappointment the man shook his head but then said, 'You'd best ask one of the waiters. I'm hardly ever in the restaurant itself.' He summoned a waiter. Hamish studied the Chinese face of the waiter, wondering if all Occidentals looked the same to oriental eyes.

But to his amazement the waiter said, 'Yes, they were here.' He put one long finger on Andrew's photograph. 'I serve them. Both times. He very good tipper.'

Privately thanking Andrew Biggar for his memorable generosity, Hamish took a statement from the waiter and got him to sign it. He felt quite scared at his own luck.

He drove happily back to Worcester, stopping at a pub on the road for a plate of sandwiches and a soft drink. He wondered whether to extend his researches on the following day by going to see Alice Brett, the legal secretary, or checking further into the Harrises, but on reflection decided that he had promised not to be away too long. He would return the hired car and go to Cheltenham and see this Mrs Agnew, inquire after Miss Gunnery's cat, and then head north.

After a substantial breakfast the following morning, he set out for Cheltenham Spa. When he got to Cheltenham, he became lost, as so many do in the one-way traffic system, and wished he had parked the car and walked. Eventually he found his way into a car park and asked directions to the terrace in which Mrs Agnew lived. The Regency spa of Cheltenham had the air almost of a seaside town. He almost expected to come to the end of a street and see the sea.

Andover Terrace was in a network of streets behind where Miss Gunnery lived. He knocked at the door of a small Georgian house wedged in between two antique shops. After some moments, the door was opened by a muscular middle-aged lady.

'Mrs Agnew?'

'Yes, but if you're selling anything, go away.'

'I have come with a message from Miss Gunnery.'

'Oh, come in, come in. What a terrible thing to happen to her. She was looking forward to a quiet holiday, too.'

Hamish followed her upstairs and into a small dark living room. Heavy carved fruit-wood furniture upholstered in red plush, the type imported from Amsterdam, was set about the room. There was a photograph of Miss Gunnery and Mrs Agnew, taken some years before. They were in tennis whites and clutching tennis rackets. Hamish nodded in the direction of the photograph. 'Are you both tennis players?'

'Were . . . were. We were both terribly keen. We both taught at the same school and played every day after school was over. So how is Felicity?'

'I think Miss Gunnery is feeling the strain. There has been another murder, you know.

'Yes, terrible, terrible. Are you a friend?'

'Of short duration. We met at the boarding-house. My name is Hamish Macbeth. I am a police constable.'

Her face hardened. 'If there is anything you want to know about Miss Gunnery, then I suggest you ask her. I have nothing to tell you.'

'I am here as a friend,' said Hamish patiently. 'She simply wanted me to tell you that she was as well as could be expected in the circumstances. I had certain things to do in Worcester and she knew Cheltenham was close. She wass verra kind to me when my dog died.' Hamish wondered whether he would always have this stab of grief when he thought of his lost pet.

'She would be. She's very sentimental about animals.'

'Miss Gunnery has a cat, I believe,' said Hamish, looking about with affected vagueness.

Mrs Agnew's eyes crinkled up in amusement. 'I know why you're here. She wanted you to check up on her cat. Joey!'

A small black-and-white cat crawled round from behind a chair. It yawned and stretched. 'There you are,' said Mrs Agnew. 'Fit and well and full of food. Tell her to look after herself and not worry about anything else. Goodness knows the poor creature has enough to worry about.' She looked at Hamish with sad eyes.

'The murders?'

'What else?' she demanded sharply.

Hamish refused an offer of tea and said he'd better be heading north.

On the long road home, he tried to think about the case but everything seemed muddled in his head. It was only when he was crossing the border into Scotland that he realized that he had not once thought of Priscilla, that she was in the Cotswolds quite near Evesham and that he could have easily visited her. Then thoughts about Doris Harris took over. She had lied by omission, as had Andrew. They had definitely known each other before and Andrew had followed her to Scotland.

Wearily giving his report to a gratified Deacon, Hamish wondered why he felt like a traitor. He handed over the waiter's statement along with the photographs.

'I don't know how you did it, laddie,' said Deacon for the second time. 'How you managed to find one restaurant where they had been seen together out o' all the restaurants around is beyond me.'

'Intuition,' said Hamish and stifled a yawn. 'I'm awfy tired and would like some sleep.'

'Aye, off wi' ye. We'll have that pair along here in the morning. Like to sit in on the questioning?'

Hamish hesitated, then reminded himself he was a policeman, and nodded.

He drove home, glad to see all the lights were out in the boarding-house. He fervently hoped that Miss Gunnery was not awake and waiting for him.

He gently unlocked the door – they had all

been supplied with keys – and eased himself into the hall. A light immediately clicked on in the lounge. He could see a strip of light under the door, hear Miss Gunnery's voice calling anxiously, 'Is that you, Hamish?'

He ran for the stairs and reached the corridor where his room was situated just as he heard the lounge door opening. He unlocked his bedroom door and plunged in, locked it behind him, and stood with his back against it, feeling like a hunted animal. He would have liked a bath, but that meant he might be waylaid on the way to the bathroom. Without putting on the light, he scrambled out of his clothes' into his pyjamas, and dived into bed just as he heard footsteps coming up the stairs. A moment later there was a quiet knock at his door and Miss Gunnery called, 'Hamish, are you there?

He let out a very stagy snore, but after another moment he heard her sigh, heard her move away. But instead of plunging down into sleep, his mind stayed resolutely restless and awake. All the people involved in the murders circulated around his brain. He began to wonder what Doris was really like. He had taken her at face value: small, neat, withdrawn, almost prim at times, putting her reserve down to the result of years of bullying. She could have left Harris. There were no children to worry about. But perhaps she had been taken 'hostage' by Harris, perhaps she had been kept down and bullied for too long to have a will or mind of her own. But what had happened to her when Andrew had entered her life? Yes, think about that, Hamish Macbeth. Andrew was gentle and mannered, the complete opposite of her boorish husband. There was the spice of secret meetings intensifying the romance. Then Harris would come back from his travels, nagging and yapping and criticizing. So what murderous thoughts began to burn in the quiet Doris's bosom? Would she not think day in and day out what her life might be if this husband were dead, and might she not discuss it with Andrew?

Then what of the beleaguered Dermott Brett and *his* secret life? He had obviously been genuine when he believed his wife would never divorce him. Harris threatened his life with June and his children. Rogers was blackmailing him. Could it be that Jamie MacPherson had been blackmailing him as well? What a crowd! Two scrubbers from Glasgow with prison records, one illicit romance, Doris and Andrew, two illicit romances if you counted Dermott and June, one unmarried schoolteacher who was in love with him . . . Hamish shuddered away from that last thought. He liked Miss Gunnery and did not want to hurt her. He twisted uneasily under the blankets and automatically leaned down to pat Towser and then remembered his dog was dead.

The death of Towser had clouded all his thoughts, making him hate the boarding-house and hate Skag and see everyone he met as a potential murderer. It was time to get to know them all again. No matter what the provocation, normal people did not kill, he firmly believed that. Somewhere, in one of them, there was the capacity to kill. And what of Alice Brett, the legitimate wife? The more he thought of her, the more anxious he became. He should have delayed his journey north and gone to see her. He must call on Deacon in the morning and ask to see a transcript of the interview with her, how much time she had taken off from work and whether she could have travelled up to Skag in time to murder Harris. But why would she *want* to murder Harris? Say he had written to her, found out her address, and written to her about June and the children. No one liked the source of bad news, but not enough to kill the bearer.

But wait a bit! He kept thinking of it as murder. The death of Harris could have been culpable homicide. Think of this. Alice goes to meet Harris. Say he suggested the jetty. He was a nasty bit of work. He would not be able to resist jeering at her. He had been drunk. Hamish could see him now, swaying slightly, his face flushed and his nag's voice going on and on. Alice seizes a piece of driftwood and whacks him on the head to shut him up. He sways and tumbles into the water. Terrified, she runs away. Then, say, Jamie MacPherson blackmails her. She has killed once, so it's easier to kill again.

But how on earth would Jamie MacPherson have got hold of her address?

Then there was that unknown quantity, Miss Gunnery. He should have dug deeper there. By saying she had slept with him, she had established a very good alibi for herself until he had broken it by telling the truth; or, to be honest, because he had been shopped by Maggie Donald. The fact was, thought Hamish ruefully, he hadn't worked hard enough.

And as if the very idea of hard work exhausted him, he fell fast asleep.

In the morning he put on his police uniform, which he had brought from Lochdubh, and made his way downstairs. Mrs Rogers stopped in the hall at the sight of him, her face suddenly contorted with fury. 'You bastard,' she hissed. 'You got my man in trouble.'

'He got himself in trouble.' Hamish looked at her coolly. 'He should ha' been more careful with a policeman in the house. He knew I wass a policeman because he searched my suitcase.'

'Havers,' said Mrs Rogers, moving away. 'Who told you that?'

'He did,' lied Hamish blandly.

She gave him a shifty look and backed towards the dining room door. 'Oh, well, we have tae check up on folks.' She went inside the dining room and slammed the door.

Hamish grinned to himself. Only a tiny part of the mystery solved, but a satisfactory one.

PC Crick came in, saw Hamish and said, 'I'm here to collect Mrs Harris and Mr Biggar. You're tae come as well.'

'I'll go ahead and see them at the station,' said Hamish, feeling squeamish at the thought of a journey with Doris and Andrew.

It was one of those still, grey days, reminding him of when he had first arrived in Skag. The sea was flat and a thin mist lay over everything.

He felt hungry but had not wanted to risk breakfast with Miss Gunnery, whose gaze on him appeared to be becoming more intense. When he arrived at the police station, Maggie was talking to Deacon in the entrance hall. 'Ah, here's Macbeth,' said Deacon. 'Get us some coffees, Maggie.' A spark of malice glinted in Hamish's hazel eyes. 'Just the thing,' he said amiably, 'and since I havenae had any breakfast, a few doughnuts would be welcome.'

'I do have police work to do,' said Maggie tartly.

'Hop to it, Constable,' snapped Deacon. 'Come along, Macbeth.'

The detective, Johnny Clay, was already in the interviewing room.

'Sit ower there, Macbeth,' said Deacon, indicating a chair in the corner.

Hamish took off his peaked cap, put it under his chair, and drew out his notebook and a stub of pencil.

'What are the reports on Alice Brett?' he asked. 'I was thinking about her. I mean, is she as hysterical as Dermott made her sound? He seemed to think she might kill herself if he asked for a divorce.'

'She's here.'

'What? In Skag?'

'We brought her up for questioning. If you want a wee look at her, we'll hae her in after we've spoken tae these two.'

The door opened. Maggie Donald put a tray with paper cups of coffee and a plate of jam doughnuts on the table. Hamish rose and helped himself, ignoring a fulminating glare from Maggie. He knew the fact that he was being allowed to sit in on the interviewing when he was only an ordinary police constable like herself had infuriated her more than being ordered to fetch doughnuts.

But when she had left, he couldn't help asking mildly, 'Doesn't it ever get up Maggie's nose, being treated like a skivvy? I mean, what about equal opportunities and no sex discrimination?'

'When that one stops trying to get favours by batting her eyelids and wiggling her bum, we'll maybe take her a bit more seriously,' said Deacon. 'And address me as "sir", when you talk to me, Macbeth.'

'Yes, sir.'

The door opened again and Doris and Andrew were ushered in. Andrew's face appeared strained and Doris looked even more buttoned down than ever, mouth tucked in at the corners, hair rigidly set, neat little blouse and straight skirt and low-heeled shoes.

'You cannot keep questioning and questioning us like this,' protested Andrew. 'We've told you all we know.'

Clay switched on the tape. 'Beginning interview with Mrs Doris Harris and Mr Andrew Biggar,' he intoned. 'Nine-fifteen, July thirtieth. Interview by Detective Chief Inspector Deacon. Also present, Detective Sergeant Clay and Constable Hamish Macbeth.'

Andrew threw Hamish a look of reproach.

'Now,' began Deacon, 'we would like to know why the pair of you omitted the fact that you both knew each other before you came up here.'

'But that's not true,' wailed Doris.

'Stop lying,' snapped Deacon. 'Look, we've gone easy on you, Mrs Harris, because of your being newly widowed and all. We have here a statement from a waiter who works in a Chinese restaurant in Evesham. He identified you from your photographs. Your fault, for being such a generous tipper, Mr Biggar. He remembered you all right. And the pair of you were seen there on two occasions. What have you to say about it?'

Doris began to cry quietly. Deacon glared at her impatiently. Andrew took Doris's hand.

'We did not lie to you,' he said quietly. 'The fact that we had met before had nothing to do with the murder investigation.'

'It seems to me it might have quite a lot to do with it,' said Deacon.

Clay leaned forward. 'So you knew each other before. So you knew, Mr Biggar, that Mr and Mrs Harris were to be here on holiday and you came along as well. Why? To put it bluntly, you could hardly have expected any romantic interludes with her husband around.' His voice hardened. 'Could it be that you came up with murder in mind?'

'I just wanted to be near her, that's all,' mumbled Andrew, looking the picture of gentlemanly embarrassment.

'We'll start again,' said Deacon. 'Were you having an affair?'

'No,' said Doris. 'Never!'

Deacon gave them both a look of patent disbelief but he said in a milder tone to Andrew, 'How did you first meet?'

'I was judging a dog show,' said Andrew. 'Afterwards I went to the refreshment tent to get a beer. When I started to leave, it was coming down in buckets. Doris was standing at the entrance to the tent. She didn't have a coat. She said something about having to wait or she would get soaked trying to reach the car park. My judging was over, so I suggested we have another drink and see if the rain eased off. We began to talk. I found her very easy to talk to.'

'Have you ever been married, Mr Biggar?' Hamish's quiet Highland lilt came from the corner of the room.

'Yes, I was married over ten years ago. She left me when I was posted to Northern Ireland. She is married again. Her married name is Hester Glad-Jones. She now lives in Cambridge. She will testify that I was never violent or abusive to her. I am not the sort to murder.'

'But you were a professional soldier until recently. You must have known how to kill men.'

'Yes, but not by hitting them on the head and pushing them in the water and leaving them to die.'

'So when did you first meet Mrs Harris?'

'I told you . . . at the dog show.'

'Yes, I know, but I want month and year.'

'It was two years ago, in August.'

'And you have been seeing each other ever since?'

'Yes, on and off. Just the occasional drink or meal. We enjoyed each other's company. There seemed no harm in it. We did not fall in love until recently.'

'You seem a sensible man to me,' said Deacon. 'Okay, I can understand you not wanting us to know that you and Mrs Harris had been seeing each other before you came up here. But for heaven's sake, man, what did you think you were doing coming up to a seedy boarding-house to watch the woman you loved being bullied by her husband? What did you think when you heard him going on at her? It drove Macbeth over there to punch Harris on the nose, although he will insist it was self-defence.'

Andrew said evenly, 'The reason I stayed was to try to persuade her to leave with me, just leave him.'

Deacon transferred his attention to Doris. 'And why didn't you?' he asked.

'I was afraid Bob would kill me.'

'But if you just went off with him, how could he find you?'

She shivered and hugged herself. 'He would have found us. I just hadn't the strength.'

Again the voice of Hamish Macbeth. 'You live with your mother, Mr Biggar. Did she know about Mrs Harris?'

He hesitated and then gave a curt 'Yes.'

'And what did she think about it? I know you are a middle-aged man, but to mothers, sons never grow up. Had she met Mrs Harris?'

'No.'

'But she knew. What did she think?'

'I do not know. I refused to discuss the matter with her.'

'You must have seen an end to this. What did you envisage?'

Andrew sighed. 'I lived from day to day. I hoped Doris would sooner or later get up the courage to leave him.'

The questioning continued. Where had they gone, apart from the Chinese restaurant, and when? At last, they were released. Maggie came in to clear away the empty cups as Deacon said to Hamish, 'Well, I think they're both mad. Why didn't they just hop into bed and have a fling?'

'You're looking at two old-fashioned people,' said Hamish. 'It struck me for the first time looking at them both that they love with the intensity of a Romeo and Juliet. They had everything against them: disapproving mother, bullying husband. But this is the real thing, this is the stuff the poets wrote about, and that's why Andrew Biggar followed her up here.'

'Havers. You're a romantic.'

'I am the realist. Some surprising people are capable of the finer feelings,' said Hamish huffily.

Maggie went out with the tray. Could Hamish Macbeth love like that? Was he right? Did that sort of love still exist when everything these days was sex, sex, sex? Perhaps she would see if he was free for dinner. That new short black skirt with the slit up the side hadn't been worn yet.

She hung about outside the interviewing room.

But Hamish was waiting inside to see Alice Brett.

Chapter Nine

Love's like the measles – all the worse when it comes late in life.
– Douglas William Jerrold

Hamish, who had been studying his notes, looked up curiously as Alice Brett was ushered in. He had expected a legal secretary to turn out to be somewhat like Doris Harris in appearance, prim and neat. But Alice Brett was fleshy. She had a loose, floppy bosom and rather big loose arms, as if they had once been muscled and the muscle had gone into flab. Her heavily painted mouth was very thick and full, and she wore an orange lipstick which had the 'wet' look, so that it was hard to look anywhere else but at that huge glistening mouth. Her eyes were large and rather fixed. She was wearing a short-sleeved summer dress. She had large plump feet in white high-heeled shoes.

Clay switched on the tape again. Deacon consulted some notes and then began. 'Mrs Brett, you say you came up here after the murder, and yet you checked out on holiday the week before. You will be interested to know that your neighbour, Mrs Dibb, now stands by her original story and has made a statement. She said you told her a week *before* the murder of Mr Harris that you had received a letter saying that your husband was cheating on you, and that you were going up to Scotland. Was that letter from Harris?'

'I want a lawyer,' said Mrs Brett.

'You'll get one. But try to co-operate. If you did not murder Mr Harris, then you have nothing to fear.'

Hamish spoke suddenly, 'The thing that is bothering me,' he said, 'was that there was hardly time for Harris to have written to Mrs Brett here. We had all been here only a few days when the murder took place.'

Deacon looked at him in surprise. Then he glared at Alice Brett. 'Out wi' it. Who told you about June?'

'I'm saying nothing until a lawyer gets here.' Alice folded her baggy arms over her baggy bosom and faced them mutinously.

And then Hamish Macbeth had one of his flashes of Highland insight.

'I know who wrote to you,' he said.

'How? Who?' asked Deacon.

'It was June,' said Hamish flatly. He looked straight at Alice Brett. 'June wrote to you, didn't she?'

She stared back and then sneered, 'Oh, well, if the silly trollop has told you, there's no point in me denying it. The bitch. Let my man go and all that crap.'

'So why didn't you approach them when you came up here?' asked Hamish. 'You weren't staying in Skag. I'm sure of that.'

'I stayed a bit away,' she said sulkily. 'I stayed in Forres. I drove over one day. You were all on the beach. It was the children. I can't have any. It made me sick. But I suddenly didn't want him any more. I went to tell him so. Of course June and the children weren't anywhere around. You know how I got my revenge? Not by murdering Harris. Why should I? I didn't know the man. I got my revenge by saying he could have had a divorce any time he wanted, and then I saw the look on his face. He was mad with fury, thinking of all the wasted years.'

'And you let him believe that you had found out about him and June through the newspapers?'

'I didn't tell him who had written to me. It didn't seem important any more.'

A possessive, ugly leech of a woman, and with another flash of insight he realized why such a woman would be prepared to let a husband go.

'You didn't much care one way or the other,' said Hamish, 'you having a new man of your own.'

'I'll kill that Dibb woman,' she shouted. 'Some friend. Can't she keep her bloody mouth shut?'

'Who is this man?' asked Deacon.

Her eyes flashed hatred in the direction of Hamish Macbeth.

'A Mr John Trant. He lives in Grays. He's a builder.'

Deacon settled down then to take her over all her movements since receiving the letter from June. She no longer said she needed a lawyer but answered in a dull, flat voice.

When they had finished with her and she had left the room, Deacon turned on Hamish. 'You might have told me all you knew about her, Macbeth,' he said. 'I've got no time for ye if you're going to be secretive.'

'I didn't know,' said Hamish mildly. 'It just came to me. Harris wouldn't know her address, and the only person I could think of who might have an interest in letting Alice know the truth was June. Also, about the other man, a creature like Alice Brett wouldn't have even considered letting Dermott have his freedom unless she had another man lined up.'

'It could be,' said Deacon slowly, 'that Brett thought Harris had written the letter.'

'But Alice arrived *after* the murder,' Clay pointed out.

'Unless, of course,' said Hamish, 'Alice met Dermott secretly before the murder. Perhaps her visit to the boarding-house was to finalize things.'

'We'd better have June and Dermott Brett in again.' Deacon rose, put his head round the door and shouted at the desk sergeant to get someone to collect them.

'Is that how you go about cases?' he asked Hamish. 'Guesswork? That can be a dangerous thing. Whit if you were wrong?'

'Then all she had to do was deny it. Seemed worth a try.'

'Aye, that's all very well, but me, I prefer solid police work and hard evidence. Just look how you came a cropper over the wrong body over at Drim.'

'But I found out the murderer,' protested Hamish. 'Look, I've been meaning to ask you. For the next few days, is there a possibility of a room in the police house at Dungarton? I don't want to go on staying at that boarding-house.'

'Why?' demanded Clay. 'You can watch them.'

'I find it a bit o' a strain,' said Hamish.

'You're a policeman, dammit.'

'But a policeman usually doesn't hae to live with the suspects.'

'You stay where you are, laddie,' said Deacon. 'Clay, give Maggie a shout and get her to make some tea and sandwiches. We'll hae a wee bit o' something while we're waiting.'

Poor Maggie, thought Hamish. If Deacon isn't careful she'll be putting in a complaint about him.

When the tea and sandwiches arrived, Hamish ate without really tasting anything, his mind on the people back at the boarding-house. He was not looking forward to the arrival of Dermott and June. He had hated being present at the interviewing of Andrew and Doris. He liked them. Why couldn't it be Cheryl or Tracey? he thought. But whoever this murderer was, it was someone cool and unemotional, or someone driven to the edge by fear. To walk into the boat-shed and kill Jamie MacPherson just like that did not seem like a premeditated crime any more than the death of Harris did. A murderer who planned things would have waited until a quieter time of the day, not marched in boldly in broad day-light, when anyone could have seen him or her. His thoughts began to wander. It could be a murderess rather than a murderer. Or was that not going to be used any more in these politically correct days? Would it soon become murderperson? Amazing that political correctness should start in a democratic society like America. One always thought of it as being the curse of a totalitarian society and coming from the top, not the bottom. Then there was therapyspeak or psychobabble to cover a multitude of emotions. People said, for example, 'I am chemically dependent on so-and-so, I am obsessed, I am emotionally dependent, I have been taken hostage.' The old-fashioned words wouldn't do any more. To go down to the basement of one's emotions, switch on the light, stare the monster in the face and say 'I am in love' was not on, because that meant giving up control, that meant being vulnerable. Had he really been in love with Priscilla? His mind shied away from the thought with all the fright of the people he had been mentally damning and he was relieved when Dermott and June were ushered in.

'Who's looking after the children?' asked Hamish and got a glare from Deacon for not knowing his place.

'Miss Gunnery,' said June.

The couple sat down uneasily and faced Deacon.

'Now,' said Deacon, 'we'll start with you, Mrs Brett. Do you mind if I call you June? I get confused with the real Mrs Brett.'

'Call me what you like,' said June wearily.

'Well, June, why didn't you tell us you had

written to Mrs Brett, telling her of your affair with Dermott here?'

Dermott's face turned a muddy colour and he stared at June as if he couldn't believe his ears. 'You WHAT?' he shouted at her.

'Quietly now,' admonished Deacon. 'I am speaking to June, not you, Dermott. June?'

'I meant to tell you,' she said, speaking to Dermott. 'I couldn't take it any longer. Eight years now we've been together. I'm sick of having you part-time. Heather was beginning to ask questions about why you had to be away so much, why you always missed Christmas, when you couldn't be working, and things like that. I thought that one day she'd find out she was a bastard and I couldn't bear that. You kept saying that Alice would never give you a divorce, but I thought she might if she knew about the children. Yes, I wrote to her. I'm not sorry. It worked out fine.'

'Except that Harris got killed and now MacPherson,' interposed Clay.

'That was nothing to do with me.'

'Wait a bit, wait a bit,' said Dermott, shaking his head as if to clear it. 'Why didn't you tell me about writing to Alice?'

'Because it would have been the same old thing,' said June. 'Look at the way you buckled and were prepared to pay that rat Rogers to keep his mouth shut.'

'But you should never have done such a thing. You don't know what you've done, woman!'

June's face turned the same horrible colour as Dermott's. 'What have I done?' she screamed at him. And then, in a low voice, she repeated wretchedly, 'Oh, what have I done?'

'Yes, what has she done?' Deacon's voice was brutal. 'Do you mean murdering Harris was a waste of time, Dermott Brett?'

'No,' said Dermott. 'I never touched him. Never! I had that row with him. He was threatening to tell Alice. I was so upset, I didn't stop to think that he couldn't possibly have the address. They don't have a visitors' book at the boarding-house.'

'Did Rogers know your home address?' asked Hamish.

'No.' Dermott quietened. 'No. June made the booking.'

'So why wass it that you told the police and us that you didn't know the boarding-house wass under the new management?'

'I lied about a few little things,' said Dermott wearily. 'I was terrified you would suspect me because I'd had that row with Harris.'

'So let's begin at the beginning,' said Deacon.

Patiently he took them through everything all over again. When he had finished, Hamish said, 'Heather says she saw Doris on the beach where Doris says she was. June, how was it you let a seven-year-old wander off on her own?'

June looked puzzled. 'It's not like Heather to leave the younger ones, but I fell asleep and Heather was collecting shells. And she was, you know. She carried them home in that pail she uses for making sand-castles.'

Maggie put her head around the door. 'A word with you, sir.'

Deacon went out. He was back in a few minutes and sat down heavily. 'More problems,' he said. 'That will be all,' he added to Dermott and June. The couple got up and went out, but Hamish noticed that Dermott did not take June's arm or hand the way he usually did.

'What's up?" asked Clay. 'Not another murder?'

Deacon shook his head. 'Cheryl's been arrested. She and Tracey were in the pub and got drunk. Some local lads started taking the piss out of them and Cheryl smashed her pint glass on the bar and then tried to take it across the face of one of the lads. Would have done it too if Tracey hadn't held her back.

Violence, thought Hamish. We've been looking for someone capable of a sudden attack of violence and forgetting Cheryl is the one with a proven record. We've been looking for a motive. What was it he had said to Miss Gunnery? Something about a motiveless murder being the most difficult to solve. These had not been intelligent murders. They had been the result of rage, rage and fear; fear in the case of MacPherson, if he had been blackmailing anybody.

Deacon was called out again. Again they waited. When he came back, he said, 'One of the locals remembers that MacPherson always had a big pair of kitchen scissors on his desk. We haven't found a trace of them. If the murderer used the scissors as a weapon and threw them in the river, they could be somewhere down there sunk in the sand. We've searched all around below the jetty, but they could have been tossed in further up. I'll tell you another thing: anything that's tossed in that river can sink down below the sand and be buried. I don't know if we'll ever find them.'

'Is Cheryl being brought in here?' asked Hamish.

'No, she'll stay in the cells until she sobers up. Why don't you get back to that boarding-house, Macbeth, and see what you can sniff out?'

That 'sniff out' was unfortunate because it gave Hamish a sudden and vivid picture of Towser. He got to his feet, nodded to Deacon and Clay, and went out. Instead of driving off, he left his Land Rover where it was and walked down to the harbour. The tide was in, sucking at the wooden piles of the jetty, making wet clumps of seaweed rise and fall like the hair on the dead Bob Harris's head. There were long trails of rain out to sea, dragging across the stormy water as if pulled by an unseen hand. The air was full of wind and salt and motion. Behind him, a policeman he did not know stood on guard outside the boat-shed. A little knot of tourists stared hungrily at the boat-shed, as if a vicarious thrill were as much a legitimate part of the holiday as the rides at the fairground.

Hamish was reluctant to go back to the boarding-house, reluctant to face the others. He wished with all his heart that the case was solved and he could return to Lochdubh. How could he ever have taken such a dislike to his home village? He could always ask to leave Skag. He was officially on holiday. But the short happy time he had spent with the others at the boarding-house before the murders had given him a queer sort of loyalty towards them.

With a little sigh, he turned and walked back to the police station, climbed into the Land Rover and drove to the boarding-house.

He was met in the hall by a stout middle-aged lady who said, 'I am Mrs Rogers's sister, Mrs Aston. Poor Liz has gone to lie down. She can't cope here. You must be Mr Macbeth. Tea is just about to be served, if you will step into the dining room.'

Wondering, Hamish went in and joined Miss Gunnery. 'I had thought of asking you out for dinner tonight,' he said. 'But do you think this Mrs Aston is going to be any better?'

'Let's see,' said Miss Gunnery. 'She seems a very civil and polite woman.'

'She seemed to have heard a description of me,' said Hamish. 'I could have been any other policeman.'

The door opened and the Bretts came in. They avoided looking at Hamish and sat down at their table in silence. Then Andrew and Doris came in, followed by a tearful Tracey. They, too, avoided looking at Hamish.

Mrs Aston wheeled in a trolley with three-tiered cake stands on it and proceeded to put one on each table. 'Goodness, this is more like it,' exclaimed Miss Gunnery. On the bottom plate were wafer-thin slices of bread and butter, white and brown; on the next plate up, teacakes and scones, golden and fresh-baked, and on the top a selection of scrumptious-looking cakes.

'I wonder what the dish is?' said Hamish. 'I smell fish and chips, but to tell the truth, I think I've had enough fish and chips to last me a lifetime.'

The trolley creaked in again. But it was fish and chips made surely by the hand of an angel: haddock fillets in crisp golden batter and real chips, rather than those frozen ones.

'This is grand!' exclaimed Hamish.

'And really good tea,' said Miss Gunnery. She looked across to where the three small Brett children sat in old-fashioned, well-behaved silence. 'There's a showing of *The Jungle Book* on in the cinema at Dungarton. It's at seven-thirty this evening. We could all just make it after tea, and it might take your children's minds off the troubles we are going through, Mrs Brett.'

'I tell you what,' said Hamish directly to the children, 'if your parents'll let you stay up late, I'll give you a ride in the police Land Rover.'

Heather's eyes widened. 'With the siren on?'

'I don't think I can manage that,' said Hamish, 'but we could flash the blue light.'

'Och, let's go,' said Tracey. 'It's started tae pour wi' rain an' if we sit in this hellish place, we'll all go daft.'

There was a definite thawing of the air in the dining room. 'Might be the very thing,' said Dermott. 'But what if they send for any of us to interrogate us again this evening?'

'They didn't say anything about it,' said Hamish. 'Let's forget our troubles and eat up and just go.'

'You'll get into trouble with your superiors for fraternizing with the enemy,' said Andrew dryly.

'Maybe Hamish hopes that if he stays close to us, we'll reveal something useful,' put in

Doris in a flat little voice. There was an uneasy silence.

'No, no,' said Hamish. 'I need to get my mind off the case as much as the lot of you. Come on. Let's give the kids a bit o' fun.'

And so Maggie Donald, arriving just after tea at the boarding-house to see if she could entice Hamish out to dinner, found him lifting the Brett children into the Land Rover. He told her rather curtly where they were going but did not issue any invitation. Maggie stood and watched as the cars drove off, feeling strangely abandoned and yet wondering crossly at the same time why Hamish Macbeth, a policeman, should want to spend the evening with a group of people among whom was probably a murderer.

The film was a great success. Hamish, who hadn't seen it before, said to Miss Gunnery that it was just about his intellectual level. Hamish drove the Brett children home and on an empty stretch of road switched on the flashing blue light and the police siren.

Miss Gunnery, following behind, driving Tracey, said, 'He is a very unusual policeman, our Hamish.'

Tracey shivered. 'They're all pigs.'

'There is nothing to fear from the police if you keep on the right side of the law,' said Miss Gunnery. 'Why don't you break free of company like Cheryl, Tracey, and make a new life for yourself?'

Tracey, instead of protesting, sat in silence. Then she said, 'She belongs to ma sort o' life. My faither's in prison.'

'There comes a time, Tracey,' said Miss Gunnery, 'when you must break free of your family if you have had an unfortunate upbringing, which I believe you have experienced.'

Tracey gave a harsh laugh. 'You know, sometimes when Ah'm comin' back frae the jiggin' wi' Cheryl, and we've had a few drinks and we're laughing and screeching, we see the respectable lassies standing at the bus stop, and they draw back a wee bit as we pass and turn their faces away. Cheryl usually gives them a mouthful, but me . . .' She sighed. 'There's a part o' me would like fine tae be one o' them.'

'You should get some skills,' said Miss Gunnery. 'Get yourself a decent job. Goodness, there are so many courses available these days. Talk to your social worker about getting a course in word processing and shorthand. Get a good job, get some digs in a good part of town. There's an awful lot you can do if you just have the courage. And it takes courage, Tracey. It takes a lot of guts, more guts than it ever takes to shoplift or get drunk. Your clothes and make-up, for example, mark you down as a vulgar tart.'

'Watch yer mouth!'

'I am giving you some straight talking. I feel there is strength and goodness in you, Tracey, that has never been tapped. You could put this horrible experience up here to good effect. You could look back on it as a watershed in your life, the day your life changed. No, don't protest. Think about it.'

Mrs Aston was waiting for them. 'Coffee in the lounge,' she announced.

'That woman is a treasure,' said Andrew as they gathered in the lounge minus June and the children, who had gone upstairs. 'I bet it isn't instant coffee either.'

The coffee was excellent. By a sort of silent agreement, no one talked about the murders, but when Hamish finally went to bed, he reminded himself severely that he was a policeman.

The next morning, Tracey was missing at breakfast. Crick, the policeman on duty, told them that Cheryl had been moved to the women's prison in Dungarton on remand and that Tracey had gone to visit her. Miss Gunnery heaved a sigh and said half to herself, 'Why did I even bother trying?'

Tracey had walked into Skag and caught the bus to Dungarton after having picked up a visitor's pass at the police station. Her hair was brushed down in a simple style and she was not wearing any make-up. She had put on a plain T-shirt, short skirt, and low-heeled shoes.

The prison was a modern one, with bullet-proof glass separating visitor from prisoner. There was a small grille to allow speech. 'How's it goin', hen?' asked Tracey.

'No' bad,' said Cheryl with a shrug. 'You're lookin' a bit plain. What hiv you done tae your hair?'

'Nothin' much,' muttered Tracey.

'Shouldnae let all this get to ye,' said Cheryl, whose hair was gelled into spikes.

'Cheryl,' ventured Tracey, 'I'm sick o' all this. I'm thinking of gettin' a career.'

Cheryl cackled with derisive laughter. 'Go on, you bampot. They cannae keep me in here fur all that long and then we'll hae a few laughs.'

'I don't want any more laughs,' said Tracey. 'I've had a fright. I want to be respectable.'

Cheryl's eyes narrowed. She could not bear to see this friend and ally slipping away. 'I've a secret to tell ye. Lean forward.'

Tracey leaned towards the glass. 'I killt them,' said Cheryl. 'Both of them.'

'Why?' mouthed Tracey silently.

'For kicks.'

Tracey got to her feet and stumbled out, her hands to her mouth. Cheryl glared after her in disbelief. There was no impressing some people.

Hamish, calling back at the boarding-house later that day after a lengthy discussion about the case with Deacon, wondered what had happened. Everyone was showing marks of strain. Tracey was a shadow of her former flamboyant self. She clung to Miss Gunnery, and Hamish wondered why such a hard piece like Tracey should suddenly decide to befriend the retired schoolteacher. But when he took Miss Gunnery aside and asked her, Miss Gunnery said that Tracey was very young and quite shaken by the murders and good might come of it. It was possible to reform anyone. Hamish looked cynical. He was sure that once Tracey was back in Glasgow with her family and friends, all thoughts of reform would go out of her head.

He returned to the police station to spend the rest of the day sifting through the statements and studying all the forensic evidence. Somewhere amongst all this pile of paper was surely a clue to the identity of the murderer. Doris and Andrew both had motives, as had June and Dermott. At last he gave up and drove into Dungarton and bought Miss Gunnery a tartan travelling-rug to replace the one in which he had buried Towser.

He gave the rug to Miss Gunnery and suggested they have dinner out that evening. Hamish was becoming worried about his dwindling finances. He felt cheated of a holiday he had initially planned to go on somewhere later in the year, but the trip south and all the other expenses had eaten into his reserves.

To his surprise, Miss Gunnery said firmly that she would pay for dinner, provided they took Tracey along with them. Hamish did not want to have any part in the reformation of young Tracey, considering her a lost cause, but felt it would be uncharitable to say so.

Like quite a lot of small Scottish towns, Dungarton boasted a Chinese restaurant in the main street, directly opposite the Indian one. It was a Saturday night and the place was quite full. Hamish looked around at the placid Scottish faces munching through crispy noodles and bean sprouts at the other tables and thought how untouched by the nasty world they all looked, safe and secure, never having known anything of the underworld stirred up by murder.

'So how was Cheryl?' he asked Tracey.

'Fine,' she said. Her hand holding the fork

trembled slightly. 'Och, when can ah go hame?' she suddenly wailed.

'Soon, I think,' said Hamish. 'The police have your home address and your statement. They'll warn you not to leave the country, and that will be that.'

'Bob Harris was a scunner,' said Tracey.

'Yes, he was,' said Hamish, 'but no one has a right to take anyone's life, Tracey.'

She stared at him with large frightened eyes, looking young and lost without her usual armour of paint and hair gel. 'Do ye believe in hell, Hamish?'

'Aye,' sighed Hamish Macbeth. 'But not in the afterlife, Tracey. We're all living in it, one way or the other, right now.'

Chapter Ten

But Guilt was my grim Chamberlain
That lighted me to bed.
–Thomas Hood

Hamish realized as he awoke next day that he had not reassured Miss Gunnery about the welfare of her cat, and what was even more strange was that she had not asked him about the cat or about her friend, Mrs Agnew.

He plunged in right away when he met her at breakfast assuring her that Joey looked fit and well. She thanked him in an abstracted voice. The murders were beginning to tell on her. Her interest in Tracey had seemed only momentarily to lift the strain. She had dark circles under her eyes and wisps of hair were escaping from her normally severe hair-style.

Everyone else seemed to be feeling equally gloomy, despite the delicious breakfast. Mrs Aston, a cheerful and motherly figure, apparently unaffected by the criminal goings-on of her sister and brother-in-law, delivered and collected plates.

'You'll be going to church,' she said to all at large.

'Good idea,' said Hamish suddenly. He was worried about the silent, downcast Brett children. Church was as good a place as any to go to on a Scottish Sabbath.

It is amazing in this modern age how such a group of normally irreligious people can suddenly decide in adversity that church is a very sensible place to go to. But then, there are no agnostics on the battlefield.

The day was quiet and calm and quite chilly when they went out to the cars, all too exhausted with worry to contemplate the walk to Skag. Crick, on duty at the door asked them where they were going and made a note of it in his book.

They arrived at the Church of Scotland in good time for the start of the service. The church was plain and devoid of ornament. They sat in one of the hard pews and listened to a wheezy organ murdering Bach.

The minister was an imposing figure, like one of the lesser prophets, with a flowing grey beard and shaggy locks. Hamish could not decide whether his eyes were burning with religious zeal or whisky. There was a strong suggestion of the actor about him. This was no clap-happy Christianity, no tambourines or steel guitars, only dreary hymns sung to the asthmatic music of the church organ.

Then the minister leaned over the pulpit and began his sermon, the theme of which was honesty being the best policy. He obviously believed more in a God of wrath than one of love and certainly appeared convinced that the dishonest were condemned to the hell of eternal fire. Without his overwhelming presence, the words would have seemed a mixture of the trite and the mad, but his voice rang round the church, conjuring up for Hamish a vision of the days of John Knox. How Mary Queen of Scots must have disliked that man!

When they emerged from the church, it was to find the weather had changed again and a hot sun was blazing down. But it was a subdued party who gathered by the cars. Tracey was weeping quietly and Miss Gunnery had an arm about her shoulders, young Heather was as white as a sheet, and Hamish cursed all Bible-bashing clerics.

They drove back to the boarding-house. I am sick of this place, thought Hamish. I want shot of it. I want to go home. And then he realized that Tracey was tugging at his sleeve. 'A word wi' ye,' she whispered. 'No' inside. Let's walk down to the beach.'

As he walked off with her, Hamish was conscious of Miss Gunnery's eyes boring into his back. For a brief spell, the spinster's interest in

Tracey had seemed to lift her growing obsession for him, Hamish. He hoped it wouldn't come back.

'What is it, then?' he asked when they had reached the shingle bank. 'Let's sit down, Tracey. You're in an awful state.'

Tracey sat down beside him, her thin white legs sticking out in front of her from under her short skirt. 'I cannae keep it tae masel' any longer,' she said. 'I know who did those murders.'

His heart beat hard against his ribs. 'Who?' he demanded sharply. 'Out wi' it!'

A glassy wave curled on to the white sand below the shingle bank.

'Cheryl,' said Tracey. 'It was Cheryl.'

He felt a great lifting of his spirits. 'How do you know?'

'She told me when I visited her in prison. She said she did it for kicks. She bragged aboot it.'

'You've got to tell the police,' said Hamish.

'You're the police!'

'I mean, them in Skag. Come on. You'll feel better when you get it over with.'

As they walked up to the boarding-house, Miss Gunnery ran to meet them. 'Is anything the matter?'

'Not now,' said Hamish. 'Later.'

He drove off to Skag with Tracey. Several times on the short journey, his heart misgave him when she muttered something to the effect of being disloyal and 'grassing' on her friend, and each time he assured her she was doing her duty.

They had to wait until Deacon and Clay were brought over from Dungarton, driven by Maggie.

In the interviewing room, Tracey, who appeared to have cried herself out, made a statement about what Cheryl had told her.

After she was led out by Maggie to wait for Hamish, Deacon said with great satisfaction, 'Thank God, that's over.'

'Aye,' said Hamish, 'you can thank God, all right. We were all at the kirk this morning and that hell-fire preacher seems to have got to Tracey. The others will be right glad and yet . . .'

He stood irresolute in the doorway.

'And yet what?' demanded Deacon testily. 'You've done a good job, Macbeth.'

All the niggling little doubts which had been replacing Hamish's initial relief came to the surface. He shook his head. 'It's too pat,' he said.

'It fits,' said Deacon. 'Cheryl's a violent criminal. She's just moved on from grievous bodily harm to murder.'

'It's the murder of MacPherson,' said Hamish. 'Think about it. What man in his right mind would try to blackmail such as Cheryl?'

'Poor old sod probably wasn't blackmailing anyone. Cheryl did the first one for kicks, so why not the second?'

'I don't like it,' said Hamish. 'It feels wrong.'

'Don't worry your head about anything, laddie. Clay and me'll go over to Dungarton and get a confession out of her.'

Hamish went outside, collected Tracey, and drove her back to the boarding-house. Miss Gunnery was waiting outside. Tracey flew to her and fell weeping into her arms. 'What's all this about?' asked Crick.

'Cheryl's confessed to the murders,' said Hamish.

'Thank heavens,' said Crick. 'Not that this hasn't become a good job, what with Mrs Aston giving me cups of tea every five minutes. Are you telling the others?'

'You tell them.' Hamish turned about and walked towards the beach over the dunes. He sat down on the shingle bank, where he had sat earlier with Tracey, and stared blindly out to sea.

How easy it would be to accept Cheryl's confession. But would she confess to the police? Had she perhaps been bragging to Tracey? Had Tracey said anything about getting free, changing her life?

Okay, June had written to Alice, a June determined to force the issue. Alice came up earlier than she had first claimed. But June had not told Dermott, and somehow Alice, who was neither a kind nor a generous-hearted woman, had let Dermott believe that she had learned the news of his adultery through the newspapers. Why? One reason was obviously because she was desperately anxious that the police should not know she had been in Skag at the time of the murder.

Dermott had quarrelled with Harris; Dermott had been blackmailed by Rogers; Dermott had lied. Doris and Andrew had lied. Yes, what about Doris and Andrew? What about all that mad burning passion that had driven one respectable upper-class Englishman to holiday in a seedy boarding-house with dreadful food so that he could be near his lady-love?

And then Hamish stiffened. There was the sound of stifled sobs coming faintly to his ears on the breeze. He got to his feet and stared around. The sound was coming from behind him, somewhere among the dunes. He walked back and stood up on top of one of the highest dunes and looked around until he caught a glimpse of white cotton to his left. He made his way there, his feet making no sound on the sand.

Heather Brett sat huddled at the foot of one of the dunes, a pathetic little figure. Sobs were racking her thin body. Hamish sat down beside her and gathered her in his arms.

'Easy, lassie,' he said. 'Easy. It's all over. What is there to cry about?'

'I-I'll burn in h-hell,' she sobbed.

'Och, you don't want tae believe what ye hear in church,' said Hamish. 'And why should the devil want a wee lassie like you, even supposing I believed in him?'

'I t-told a bad lie,' whispered Heather.

Hamish held her closer. 'Every human being lies some time or the other, Heather. You can tell me.' He took a handkerchief out of his pocket and dried her face. 'Now then, nobody's going to get angry with you. I'll see to that. What lie?'

She gave a little tired sigh. 'I didn't see Mrs Harris on the beach.'

He stiffened. 'Why did you say so?'

'I promised them I would.'

'Them?'

She began to cry again. Hamish felt a great wave of fury. Using a child like this!

He lifted her to her feet. 'Come along,' he said. 'It'll be all right. I'll explain matters. Mrs Harris had no right to ask you to lie. And don't you be worrying about hell-fire. Nothing's going to happen to you. You're a good wee lassie, Heather.' And coaxing and cajoling, he led her back over the dunes to where a worried June came running to meet them.

'Take care of your daughter,' said Hamish. 'She told a lie to the police, but it's not her fault. I'll go and see Deacon right now. Where's Andrew and Doris?'

'They went into the pub in Skag, but –'

'Later,' said Hamish. He ran to his Land Rover, jumped in and drove straight to the pub. Andrew and Doris were sitting at a table in a corner over a plate of sandwiches and glasses of beer.

'The pair of you are in bad trouble,' said Hamish grimly.

'Why?' Andrew looked surprised. 'As a matter of fact, we were having a small celebration. Cheryl's confessed.'

Hamish ignored that. 'Why did you persuade that child, Heather, that you were on the beach on the day of the murder? Why did you get her to lie?'

'You're talking rubbish,' shouted Andrew. A few locals turned and stared at them in surprise. 'Rubbish,' he repeated in a lower voice. 'No one told Heather to say anything. We didn't tell her to lie.'

Doris sat with her head bent. 'Doris?' prompted Hamish.

'I meant it for the best,' she said. 'Everyone would think it was me. I meant to put it straight.'

Hamish looked at the horrified surprise on Andrew's face and said, 'Them. Heather said "them". They had told her to lie. I assumed it was you and Andrew. Who was the other one, Doris?'

She looked at him pleadingly.

'Miss Gunnery.'

'*What!*'

'She was most sympathetic about Andrew and me. She said the police always suspected the wife, so it was important for me to have an alibi. She said Heather wouldn't mind lying. She said she had always found that children were natural-born liars.'

'You'll need to make a statement. You'll need to correct your earlier statement. Where were you, Doris? I myself saw you going towards Skag.'

'I was so miserable, I just walked about,' said Doris. 'I don't think anyone saw me. I didn't have any alibi. Miss Gunnery said it was imperative that I have one.'

'I can't believe it of you, Doris,' said Andrew angrily. 'The police could charge you for wasting their time. It's just as well for you that Cheryl has confessed.'

'If she has confessed,' said Hamish heavily. 'We've only got Tracey's word for it at the moment. Wait here. Let me speak to Deacon first. If Cheryl has really confessed and they have some positive proof she did the murders, because a confession alone is not enough in Scotland, there'll be no need for me to say anything.'

He went to the police station to learn that Deacon and Clay were still at the prison in Dungarton. Maggie, who gave him the news, looked at him curiously. 'You look terrible. I thought you'd be glad it was all over.'

'I need a phone,' said Hamish, walking towards the interview room.

'You'll need permission . . .' began Maggie, but Hamish walked in and slammed the door behind him.

He sat down at the desk and stared at the phone. Think. Twice Miss Gunnery had lied, or rather, she had lied once and then engineered it that Heather should lie to protect Doris. An image of the photograph of Miss Gunnery and Mrs Agnew came into his head. He took out his notebook and found the slip of paper with Mrs Agnew's address. He dialled directory inquiries and asked for her phone number. What was it Mrs Agnew had said? 'Goodness knows, the poor creature has enough to worry about.' And looking back, he remembered having a feeling that Mrs Agnew had not been talking about the murders, but about something else.

When she answered the phone, he said, 'Mrs Agnew, this is Police Constable Hamish Macbeth. It is verra important for Miss Gunnery's sake that you tell me the truth. Was something worrying her?'

'Of course something was worrying her,' said Mrs Agnew tartly. 'Aren't two murders enough to worry anyone? How is she? Alive?'

'Yes, why shouldn't she be? Look, Mrs Agnew, if you know anything about Miss Gunnery that bears any relation on this case, then it is your duty to tell me.'

'I know nothing that bears any relation to the murders. Nor does she.'

'Well, for heffen's sake, woman, what's the other thing that's worrying her? I'll find out, if not from you, then from anyone else that knows her!'

'Oh, if it stops you poking around . . . Poor Felicity has only a few months left to live. She has cancer and she should be back here attending the hospital.'

He stared at the phone receiver. Then he said slowly, 'Was Miss Gunnery ever married?'

'No, no.'

He thought of Doris and Andrew, feeling with his mind for the right questions to ask, feeling blindly. 'Was she effer in love wi' anyone?'

'Really, Mr Macbeth –'

'Chust answer the damn question!' he shouted.

'I do not see what it has to do with anything. Yes, a few years ago, when we were both teaching at Saint Charles, she fell in love with the geography teacher, a much younger man, and a married one, too.'

'So what came of it?'

'Nothing. The man was married.'

'Thank you, Mrs Agnew. I'll get back to you if there's anything else.'

He replaced the receiver.

Miss Gunnery, dying of cancer, disappointed in love. He would need to talk to her.

He left the police station and drove off to the boarding-house.

Deacon came back shortly after Hamish had left, his face set in grim lines. 'Did she confess, sir?' asked Maggie eagerly.

'Aye,' said Deacon bitterly. 'The wee bitch confessed to lying to Tracey, and that's all we've got. Back to square one. I'll hae that lot back along here, one by one. But after I've had some tea. See to it, there's a good girl.'

'Hamish Macbeth was here, sir,' said Maggie, fighting down a desire to scream at him to get his own tea.

Deacon, who had been walking away, swung round. 'What did he want?'

'I don't know. He used the phone in the interview room.'

'Who to?'

'He didn't tell me.'

'We'll have that one back as well. He's not living up tae his reputation.'

Hamish Macbeth went into the lounge. They were all gathered there. He looked bleakly at all of them: June and Dermott and the children, Doris and Andrew, Miss Gunnery and Tracey.

He stood in front of the fireplace and then he said quietly to Miss Gunnery. 'You've got some explaining to do.'

She gave a nervous laugh. 'Oh, Heather told me about telling you about that lie. But no harm's done. Cheryl's confessed.'

'I haven't heard from Deacon, but Cheryl only bragged to Tracey about committing the murders. If she sticks to her story, I'll be surprised. So let's say it wasn't her. It wass the one of you.'

They stared at him, hypnotized.

'I'm going to speculate. Here's what I think happened:

'Miss Gunnery, you have been disappointed in love, and that very disappointment made your eyes sharper than mine. You knew that Doris and Andrew were really in love, passionately in love. Harris was a hateful man. You longed to help. Quite what happened, I don't know. But perhaps you came across Harris and tried to reason with him. He had a vile tongue. Did he insult you drunkenly and then turn away in contempt? Was that when you struck him with those arms strengthened by the years of tennis playing? Anyway, you left him to die in the water. Then you began to try to cover not only your own tracks by saying you had slept wi' me, but you clumsily tried to protect Doris by using a wee child.

'You havenae long to live, Miss Gunnery, and I think that prompted you. By the time they found out anything, *if* they found out anything, with any luck you'd be dead. But you havenae helped anyone. All you've done is brought misery all round. Doris here is haunted wi' the idea that Andrew might hae done it, and he sometimes worries about her.' He looked at Doris. 'Isn't that true?'

'Yes,' said Doris faintly.

'Then, as I see it, MacPherson turns up and starts to blackmail you, Miss Gunnery. He wouldnae have bothered trying to blackmail someone like Cheryl. So you stabbed him with the scissors on his desk. Luck was on your side. No one saw you. No one ever really sees you, Miss Gunnery. That was the story of your life, was it not? A shadow, a cipher, passed over and ignored. And the one time love came into your life, it had to be a married man who wouldn't leave his wife.'

His voice had taken on an uncharacteristically cruel and jeering edge.

She put her hands up as if to ward him off. 'I meant it for the best,' she said. 'It was only for the best. Henry's wife was a bully and a nag –'

'Henry being the geography teacher.'

She nodded. Then she rallied. 'You have no proof . . . no proof. Who's going to believe you?'

Hamish sat down suddenly in a chair by the fireplace. 'I'll bet you have the proof hidden away somewhere,' he said in a tired voice. 'It would be like you to keep something for insurance chust in case someone innocent was accused of the murder, someone other than Cheryl, that is. You wouldn't care much about Cheryl. But you're a romantic. You did it all for Doris and Andrew. Where you had failed in love, they must not fail. I must be losing my wits. June, take the kids away.'

June marshalled her brood and took them out. Hamish jerked his head at Dermott. 'Go with them.'

He turned back and said almost pleadingly to Miss Gunnery, 'You know me. I'll dig and pester and dig and pester and I'll neffer leave you alone. If you want Doris and Andrew to be free, then admit your crimes. You wanted to be found out, didn't you? You sent me to see your friend in Cheltenham. You had probably told her not to tell anyone that your life was shortly to end. You didn't show much interest in your cat, didn't even ask me when I came back. Oh, you didn't sit down and think, if I ask Hamish Macbeth to call in on Mrs Agnew in Cheltenham, he might find out something about me. It wasn't as clear-cut as that. What stopped me from suspecting you was because I liked you and could see no motive. I remember saying to you that a motiveless crime was the best one. Then there was the death of MacPherson. It took some force to drive those scissors into his neck. I'd neffer really noticed the strength of your arms before. Then I remembered that photo of you and Mrs Agnew in your tennis whites.'

She got to her feet. 'Your reasoning is hardly logical,' she said, 'and as you know, there is no proof.' Her voice shook. 'I will go to my room and lie down. All this has been too much for me.' She went out and Hamish could think of no concrete reason to stop her.

'It cannae be her,' wailed Tracey. 'The only decent body who's ever been kind tae me.'

'Are you sure, Hamish?' asked Andrew. 'Why not phone Deacon and see if Cheryl has confessed?'

'She didn't protest all that much,' said Doris. 'If she'd been innocent, surely she would have shouted at Hamish and threatened to report him to his superiors. Then she did say she had done it for the best.'

Mrs Aston put her head around the door. 'Coffee?' she asked brightly.

'Aye, that'll be chust grand,' said Hamish.

'I'll bring a tray in. I'll put an extra cup on it for Miss Gunnery. Maybe she'll be feeling like one when she gets back from the beach.'

Hamish jumped to his feet. 'The what? She's gone out?'

'I think she must have forgotten something. She went off running.'

'Didn't Crick stop her?'

'He's in the kitchen having his coffee.'

Hamish ran out of the room, out of the boarding-house and over the dunes to the beach. He looked right and left when he reached the beach and then out to sea. Far out, bobbing above the waves, he could see a head.

He stripped down to his underwear and plunged in and started swimming powerfully. The wind was rising and the waves were rising and he battled through one after the other.

At last he saw her some yards in front of him and called loudly to her. She saw him, rather than heard him, for the wind whipped his words away. She was still wearing her glasses. How odd, he thought madly, that her glasses had managed to stay on. The sun glinted on them, giving her a blind look. Then she raised her arms to heaven and sank under the waves like a stone.

* * *

Deacon and Clay had been phoned by Crick. They had come with Maggie and, joined by Dermott, Tracey, Andrew and Doris, they stood on the edge of the water and watched as Hamish struggled back, holding Miss Gunnery in his arms.

Clay and Crick waded in to help him as he neared the shore. Together they carried Miss Gunnery's limp body on to the sand. Maggie moved in and began applying all the artificial respiration techniques she had learned. Far away sounded the wail of an ambulance siren. At last, Maggie sat back on her heels and shook her head.

'She's dead,' she said flatly.

The wind rose even higher, the white sand snaked along the beach and began to sing a dirge for Miss Gunnery.

'So let's have it then,' said Deacon to Hamish. 'Mr Biggar here says you accused Miss Gunnery of the murders. What proof had you?'

'None,' said Hamish, pulling his dry clothes over his wet underwear. 'Chust intuition.'

'Oh, shite, man. If you've driven that lady to her death by your harassment . . .'

'She'll hae left proof somewhere,' said Hamish wearily. 'And I'm going to look for it.'

'You won't find it,' Deacon shouted at his retreating back. 'Don't you know all the rooms were searched several times?'

Deacon waited until the ambulance men arrived, until he had had a full report from Andrew about what had happened in the lounge before Miss Gunnery had swum to her death, before setting off in pursuit of Hamish.

'That Blair ower in Strathbane was right,' he grumbled. 'Hamish Macbeth is stark-staring mad.'

Hamish sat on the bed in Miss Gunnery's room and looked about him. He was bone-weary. He had had to dive and dive before he had managed to get her. He had searched already, but there was nothing in her suitcase, or in the drawers, or in the bedside table. Then he thought: the police had not been looking for drugs, so their search would only have been through her belongings. So where would be the obvious place? He rolled back the carpet, but the floorboards did not seem to have been disturbed. Then he went out and went along to the communal bathroom. The toilet had an old-fashioned cistern, the type that is set high up, with a chain dangling from it. He stood on the pan and lifted the lid of the cistern. Nothing in the cistern, he thought, feeling around with his hand. And then, because he was so very tired, as he was about to replace the lid, it slipped out of his hands and fell on the floor. And there, staring up at him, taped to the underside of the cistern lid, was an oilskin packet.

He climbed down, sat on the floor, and ripped the packet free, wondering vaguely where, in this day and age of plastic, Miss Gunnery had been able to find oilskin. And for one moment, before he opened the packet, he wondered if it might turn out to have nothing to do with Miss Gunnery but was something criminal hidden by Rogers.

But on opening it he found two envelopes. One was addressed to himself.

He opened it.

'Dear Hamish Macbeth,' he read, 'In the event of anyone being falsely accused for the murders, I have written this confession of what I have done.'

He had a feeling of relief as he read on. The murder of Harris had been on impulse. Miss Gunnery had come across him that day in Skag. She had pleaded with him to give Doris her freedom. She had told him she knew what it was like to be in love. He had made several crude remarks about her lack of any attraction, called her a warped little spinster, and turned away. She had picked up the driftwood and hit him with it as he stood at the edge of the jetty. When he had fallen in the water, she had been about to run for help. But then she had thought of Doris and Andrew. She, Miss Gunnery, did not believe in God or divine retribution. As far as she was concerned, she was soon to die, and that would be the end of everything. So why not just let Harris die? Furthermore, she herself might be sent to prison for assault and she had no intention of spending her remaining days behind bars. So she had left him and then had done her clumsy best to see that no one else should suffer. Then MacPherson had approached her, said he had seen her and demanded money. She told him she would pay him. But, she had written in that old-fashioned italic writing so rarely seen these days, she felt that he did not deserve to live either. So she had gone quietly into his shed when he was working at his desk, seized up the scissors and driven them into his neck. The scissors were wrapped in a plastic bag and buried under the lilac tree in the garden of the boarding-house at the back. Her fingerprints would be found on them. 'I did not lie about sleeping with you to give myself an alibi, Hamish,' she ended, 'but to give you one because I love you.'

Hamish put it down on the floor and opened the other envelope. It contained a will form. Miss Gunnery had left everything she owned to Tracey.

Chapter Eleven

What beck'ning ghost along the moon-light shade
Invites my steps, and points to yonder glade?
– Alexander Pope

The following morning, Hamish sat for the last time in the interview room with Deacon. Clay had been sent out.

'Now,' began Deacon, 'take me over it again. Why did you suddenly come to the conclusion that a woman like Miss Gunnery had committed two murders?'

'I had been feeling uneasy about her for some time,' said Hamish, 'but I thought that was because she was falling in love wi' me. It stopped me from thinking about her too much. And she seemed so kind. Kind to me over the death of my dog, kind to the Brett children, kind to Tracey. You could say that it was that kindness that killed Harris. She thought she was giving Doris all the love and new life that she had been cheated of herself.'

'I told you – a repressed spinster,' said Deacon.

'I still don't agree wi' ye. There's folks these days won't even use the word "spinster", it's become such an insult. What woman these days is even still a virgin at her age?'

'She was,' said Deacon with satisfaction. 'Preliminary pathologist's report.'

'Oh, well,' said Hamish huffily, 'if ye knew all about it, why didn't you suspect her yourself?'

'Now, now, I'm not saying you haven't been clever. But what made you think of her?'

'It was when I learned she had made Heather tell that lie. I was uneasy about Cheryl's supposed confession. I realized I hadn't been thinking clearly about her. There were all sorts of little things: lying about having been in bed with me; telling me to look up her friend in Cheltenham and ask about her cat and then not showing any interest in the animal when I came back; her friend implying that she was worried about something other than the murders; and then there was a photograph of her and her friend in their tennis whites. I remembered seeing Miss Gunnery in her swimsuit and noticing she had very strong forearms, although it didn't register at the time. I realized that, desperate and strong enough, she could have stabbed MacPherson with the necessary force. You found the scissors?'

'Aye, right where she said they would be. We've sent them off to be checked for fingerprints. But what could you have done had she stuck to her original story, said she was innocent?'

'I would ha' got you to pull Doris in and then tell Miss Gunnery she had been charged with the murder and, worn down with brutal police questioning, she had confessed and was talking about taking her own life.'

'You're a ruthless man, Macbeth. Wouldnae think it to look at you.'

'I can't be doin' wi' murder,' said Hamish severely. 'Mind you, I'm feeling rather stupid. There I was having dinner and making friends with a woman who must have been as mad as a hatter and I didnae suspect a thing.'

'Well, you got a result anyway.' Deacon picked up a paper-knife and twisted it this way and that. 'You'll be off to Lochdubh today.'

'I suppose so.'

'When?'

'I don't know when,' said Hamish testily. 'Does it matter?'

Clay put his head round the door. 'The press are arriving.'

Hamish leaned back in his chair and smiled. 'Giving a press conference, sir?'

'Aye, well, I called one,' said Deacon gruffly. 'If you'd like to give me a list of your expenses, I'll see they go through.'

'I have them right here,' said Hamish, handing them over.

'Goodbye then,' Deacon stood up.

Hamish remained sitting. 'Och, I think I might as well stay for that press conference of yours.'

'Off with you, Clay,' snapped Deacon. Clay withdrew his head and closed the door.

Deacon sat down again and pulled open a desk drawer and took out an envelope. 'Since your holiday was spoiled working for me, Macbeth, I thought the enclosed might compensate you.'

Hamish opened the envelope. Inside it were four fifty-pound bank notes. How dare you bribe a police officer? was his first thought, followed by the more pragmatic one that a bribe from a superior to an inferior could really hardly be called a bribe . . . could it?

He stuffed the envelope in his trousers pocket and stood up. 'I'll be off then, sir.'

Deacon smiled his relief.

'Call in and see us any time, Macbeth.'

When Hamish had left, Deacon went to a small mirror in the corner, carefully brushed his hair, straightened his tie, and then went off to tell the press how he had solved the murders.

Hamish returned to the boarding-house. They were gathered in the lounge. Andrew appeared to be advising Tracey on how to go about claiming her legacy. Tracey looked elated. The others appeared relaxed and relieved. Poor Miss Gunnery! No one to mourn her, thought Hamish, and then wondered why he should even think such a thing. Miss Gunnery had taken two lives, and had escaped both a lingering death and the full weight of the law.

'I suppose we're all going home,' said Hamish.

'Oh, yes,' began Doris eagerly.

'Don't interrupt me, Doris,' said Andrew severely. 'I have just been telling Tracey here it is important that she does not tell either Cheryl or her family of her legacy. Doris and I will take her south with us to Cheltenham and find her a lawyer. You may repay us when you get your legacy, Tracey. Just write to your family saying we have invited you to go with us on an extended holiday.'

'Oh, aye, Ah'll do that,' said Tracey eagerly.

Hamish looked curiously at Doris's face, which when Andrew had admonished her had momentarily had that closed look it had worn when her late husband had been nagging her.

Heather was playing quietly with her brother and sister in the corner. She looked recovered from her ordeal. Hamish felt very weary and grubby.

He excused himself and went upstairs and had a bath and changed. He took himself off to Dungarton for dinner, not wanting to go to the dining room and sit opposite Miss Gunnery's empty chair.

He noticed when he drove back that it was once more dark at night in the north of Scotland. As he approached Skag, he saw a couple with their arms wrapped about each other walking by the side of the road. His headlamps picked them out – Deacon and Maggie, walking as close as lovers. Well, I never! he thought crossly. That one's determined to get promotion any way she can!

He parked the police Land Rover outside. He wondered if the others had left. He himself would have one more night's sleep at The Friendly House. He switched off the engine and climbed out.

And then he heard barking from the beach. His heart gave a jolt. The barking sounded like Towser's. He turned and ran towards the beach, stumbling over the dunes towards the sound of that joyful barking.

He could make out the dim shape of a large mongrel running along by the edge of the curling waves.

'Towser!' he shouted.

And then there was nothing there, nothing at all but the waves curling in the moonlight, the hissing sand, and the empty beach.

He walked slowly back, realizing he was so very tired, he must have been hallucinating.

On the other hand, it would be comfortable to think that somewhere there was another world for dead pets where they were happy and that he had briefly had a glimpse of it.

He let himself in and went up the stairs, undressed and plunged gratefully into bed, without even bothering to wash or clean his teeth.

He awoke in the morning to a sunny day, washed and dressed and went down to the dining room.

To his surprise they were all still there. 'We all decided it would be best to set off after breakfast,' said Andrew. 'Have you got everything packed in the cars, Doris?'

'Yes, dear.'

'So I'll take Tracey and you follow us.'

'I hope I'll be all right,' said Doris timidly. 'I've never driven such a long way on my own before.'

'You'll be all right,' said Andrew.

After breakfast, they all shook hands and exchanged addresses, just like any normal holiday-makers. Hamish was the first to leave. They stood in a little group outside, waving goodbye to him.

He wondered if he would ever see any of them again.

* * *

The hills were ablaze with purple heather as he drove down the heathery track into Lochdubh. Willie, polishing the brass doorknob outside the restaurant, turned and waved. The sun sparkled on the sea loch, the fishing boats rode at anchor, and seagulls sailed overhead against the bluest of skies.

He was home at last and felt he had been away from Lochdubh for years.

He opened up the police station, took the sign off the door which referred all inquiries to Sergeant Macgregor at Cnothan, lit the stove, and began to go about the pressing duties of gardening and tending to his livestock. During the day, villagers called round to stand and chat.

It was only as evening approached that he realized he had not inquired after Priscilla. He was free of that at last and yet he did not know whether to be glad or sorry.

No Towser, no Priscilla, the start of a new chapter in his life.

Dr Brodie and Angela called and took him out for dinner at the Italian restaurant where the servings were back to their normal generous size, the owner having returned from Italy and put an end to Willie Lamont's parsimony. As Hamish told them about the case, the more faraway and unreal it seemed in his head.

'You're usually so sharp about people,' said Angela. 'I'm surprised you didn't think there might be something badly wrong in the character of this Miss Gunnery.'

'I've often thought about it,' said Hamish. 'She seemed that kind, and I was thrown by Towser's death. She must have been quite mad. I tell you, there's something weird about Skag – so flat, all those singing sands.' He fell silent. He had been so anxious to leave that he had not even called on old Miss Blane again, as he had promised he would.

'Do you think this Tracey will really reform? What was left to her by Miss Gunnery?'

'I don't really know,' said Hamish. 'Andrew Biggar was going to look into it. A tidy bit, I should guess. Then there would be the flat in Cheltenham. Perhaps, once the euphoria of being home is over, Andrew and Doris will drop her.'

'And do you think Andrew and Doris will live happily ever after?' asked Angela.

'That I don't know. Doris is one o' those women who can make men into bullies, not that I'm saying that Harris wasn't a rat. And how will Doris cope with Andrew's mother? She's a big, bossy sort of woman. As long as they don't live wi' her, it'll probably muddle along all right.'

At the end of the meal, he thanked them and walked home. Great stars were burning overhead and there was a cold nip in the air.

He would put the whole Skag experience behind him. He would probably never hear anything about any of them again.

The following February, Hamish came indoors from shovelling snow away from the police station path to hear the phone in the office ringing.

Hoping he would not have to go out in such filthy weather to deal with some crime, he answered it. To his surprise, it was the editor of the Worcester newspaper he had phoned the summer before for information about Andrew.

'I wondered whether you were still working on that case,' said the editor.

'Och, no, that was solved and over last summer,' said Hamish, thinking not for the first time that it always came as a bit of a jolt to realize that what appeared world-shattering in the far north of Scotland did not even cause a ripple in the south of England.

'Oh, well, it was just that a bit of news about that Andrew Biggar arrived on my desk.'

'What's that?'

'He's getting married.'

'Oh, well, that was on the cards . . . to Doris Harris.'

'You know? Wait a bit. That wasn't the name. Where is the damn thing?' There was the sound of an impatient rustling of papers.

'Here it is. No, he's marrying someone called Tracey Fink. Still, it's no use to you now.'

'No, no use now,' said Hamish slowly. He thanked the editor and replaced the phone.

It had all been for nothing. Two murders committed so that Romeo and Juliet in the form of Andrew and Doris could enjoy the great love they had for each other. Gentleman Andrew and slaggy Tracey. They would need a board with subtitles at the wedding so that the English guests could make out what she was saying, he thought cynically. What on earth had happened?

Probably the middle-aged Andrew had found it delightful to act as Pygmalion to the coarse Tracey, the young Tracey, while timid Doris became a bore.

Perhaps what had sparked the love between Doris and Andrew had been the secrecy of their meetings. The minute the way lay clear to marriage, he might have begun to find her irritating.

What a waste of life, and all in the name of love!

I hope there is an afterlife, thought Hamish savagely, and I hope, Miss Gunnery, you're seeing and hearing everything.

He poured himself a glass of whisky from a drawer in his desk. This year, he should go on holiday somewhere or another. But he would probably stay in Lochdubh and go fishing.

The world outside was a wicked place.

If you enjoyed *Death of a Nag*, read on for the first chapter of the next book in the *Hamish Macbeth* series . . .

DEATH of a MACHO MAN

Chapter One

. . . When two strong men stand face to face,
Though they come from the ends of the earth.
– Rudyard Kipling

Randy Duggan was called the Macho Man in the village of Lochdubh in the Scottish Highlands and he seemed to live up to his nickname. He was a huge man, over six feet tall, with powerful shoulders, tattoos and a low forehead. His legs were disproportionally short for his body and his hair was greasy and worn long and curly on his collar. He wore leather jackets with long fringes. He sported odd glasses with slats like venetian blinds, and brightly coloured hats. The locals gathered in the Lochdubh bar just to see him crush beer cans in one of his great fists. His voice had an American twang. He said he had been a wrestler in America.

In fact, to the admiring locals, it seemed as if Randy had been everywhere, seen everything, done everything. He had been attacked by muggers in Florida, shot them dead, and had been commended by the police for his bravery. He had been a lumberjack in Canada and he had shot a bear in Alaska. He was the most well-travelled man Lochdubh had ever seen.

It was all too easy to create a sensation in Lochdubh. It was a sleepy Highland village in Sutherland, which is as far north as you can go on the mainland of the British Isles. Tourists came and went in the summer season, but not many, most of them only getting as far north as Inverness.

Perhaps, in the easygoing way of the Highlanders, they would have accepted Randy at face value, and being prime liars and tall storytellers themselves, were not given to picking holes in anyone's anecdotes, least of all their own. And if Randy had never been faced with any criticism or competition, things might have gone on the way they were and not turned nasty.

Of course, the weather contributed to the edginess that was created in the Lochdubh bar one day when Randy, as usual, was holding forth. The other reason for his admiring audience was that Randy was free with his money, and fisherman Archie Maclean, one of Randy's best listeners, had been barely sober since the big man had arrived in the village, such was Randy's generosity to this, his best admirer.

It was another day of irritating rain and drizzle. Long trails of rain dragged in from the Atlantic and up the sea loch outside the bar. Midges, those maddening Highland mosquitoes, were out in black clouds, no rain seeming to deter them. The atmosphere was muggy and close. It was the tenth day of rain and the damp permeated everything and clothes stuck to the body, and where the clothes did not stick, the midges stung with savage fury. Patel's, the general store, had run out of midge repellent only that day.

Randy had geographically moved to the Middle East in his tales. Little Geordie Mackenzie, a retired schoolteacher, brightened up. He was normally shy and retiring. He had recently moved to Lochdubh and had not yet made any friends. When Randy paused in an account of dining in a Bedouin tent to take another swig of beer, Geordie piped up in a reedy voice, 'I was out in Libya during my National Service, and a very odd thing happened to me when we were out on manoeuvres in the desert . . .'

But no one was destined to hear what had happened to Geordie in the desert, for the Macho Man glared at the schoolteacher and raised his voice. No one could tell him anything about adventures in the Middle East. He had eaten sheep's eyes and run an illegal still in Saudi Arabia and had been thrown in prison in Riyadh, escaping his jailers the day before his hand was due to get chopped off.

Geordie looked crushed and put down. Archie Maclean began to feel irritated with Randy. The big man could have let wee Geordie have his say. The air of the bar was stuffy with cigarette smoke, his wife was a mighty washer and cleaner and the collar of his starched shirt was rubbing against the mosquito bites on his neck. He saw Geordie creeping out of the bar and followed him.

'Don't pay him nae heed,' said Archie, catching up with Geordie. 'He likes his crack.'

'He's a braggatt and a liar,' said Geordie primly. 'I don't believe any of his stories.'

'I'm getting pretty tired o' him mysel',' said Archie. 'We used to all sit around and have a wee bit o' a gossip. Now we all hae tae listen tae that big tumshie, blethering on and on and on. Damn thae midges. They've got the teeth of them like razors this year. Oh, here's our local bobby. D'ye ken Macbeth?'

'I have seen the constable about the village but have not yet spoken to him,' said Geordie.

'Hey, Macbeth!' called Archie. 'Come and meet the latest incomer.'

They had reached the harbour, where fishing boats rose and fell at anchor on an oily swell. It was Sunday, the Lord's day, which meant the bar might be open but taking a fishing boat out was flying in the face of Providence.

Hamish Macbeth, Lochdubh's police constable, was ambling along the waterfront towards them. He was a tall, lanky Highlander with flaming red hair, a thin, sensitive face and hazel eyes. Geordie judged him to be in his mid-thirties.

'This here is Geordie Mackenzie,' said Archie. 'He's just moved in tae Lochdubh.'

'Aye, I know,' said Hamish. His voice had a Highland lilt. 'You've taken thon cottage up the hill a bit behind the Curries. Where did you come from?'

'Inverness, Mr Macbeth.'

'Hamish,' said the policeman. 'I'm called Hamish.'

He gave a gentle smile and the lonely Geordie felt warmed by it. 'Hamish, it is. I've just left the bar over there, Hamish, because I cannot stand the lies and bragging of that Randy Duggan any more.'

'No harm in a few lies,' said Hamish easily. He told quite a lot himself. 'You don't have to listen.'

'Oh, but I do!' said Geordie, burning with resentment all over again. 'His voice fair dominates the bar.'

'Aye, I suppose it does. But so long as he's paying for the drinks,' said Hamish, 'there'll always be folk to listen. Isn't that right, Archie?'

'Och, weel.' Archie shuffled his feet. 'It was a wee bit o' fun at first, but now it's too much, but ye can hardly tell a fellow o' that size tae shut up.'

'Now that's where you're wrong,' said Geordie eagerly. He was emboldened by this friendly conversation. 'He hasn't often come up against an educated man before, of that I am certain.'

Hamish looked amused. 'We are not all village peasants, Geordie.'

'I'm sorry,' said Geordie quickly, 'I didn't mean to be rude. But someone should stand up to him.'

'Och, be careful, man,' cautioned Hamish. 'The further away a man gets from his last fight, the braver he gets. I have a feeling in my bones that thon Randy could be a nasty customer.'

'I think he's all wind and bluster,' said Geordie.

Hamish studied the little man thoughtfully. Geordie, he thought, must be in his late sixties and had probably never been in a fight since he was a schoolboy. Hamish was lazy. He smelt trouble coming but was reluctant to make any effort to stop it. Randy Duggan had appeared out of the blue a few weeks ago. He had tried to book into the Tommel Castle Hotel, but Colonel Halburton-Smythe, the owner, had taken one horrified look at him and said there were no vacancies. Randy had rented a holiday cottage up on the hill near Geordie's. The colonel had reported various spiteful attacks of vandalism; fences cut, the back wall of the hotel spray-painted with a large four-letter word, and the windows of the gift shop broken. Hamish wondered whether Duggan, the Macho Man, was taking his spite out on the colonel but, as yet, he had no proof. Hamish was beginning to think that the big man was a phoney. In his cups, his accent slipped and became more Scottish than American. But until he found something to drive Duggan out of Lochdubh or some proof so that he could arrest him for vandalism, all he could think to do was to try to defuse what he was rapidly beginning to see as an explosive situation.

'It would maybe be the best thing to take Randy Duggan's audience away from him,' said Hamish.

'Drink somewhere else?' Archie looked at the policeman in surprise. 'There isnae anywhere else to drink.'

'There's that bar at the Tommel Castle Hotel,' said Hamish. 'That's open to non-residents.'

'That's posh,' said Archie. 'Come on, Hamish. Ye cannae see a bunch o' fishermen and forestry workers up there. The colonel would be spittin' blood.'

'Think about it,' said Hamish. 'It would only be for a wee bit.'

'I'm game,' said Geordie eagerly.

Hamish pushed his cap back on his fiery hair. 'It's a quiet season. The colonel should be right glad o' the trade.'

Priscilla Halburton-Smythe, the cool and stately blonde daughter of Colonel Halburton-Smythe, had recently returned from London and was once more running the gift shop. She had at one time been briefly and unofficially engaged to Hamish Macbeth, and since the end of their romance had kept out of his way. She therefore found it irritating when her father summoned her and suggested she call on Hamish to ask for help.

'More vandalism?' asked Priscilla. 'You can deal with that yourself, Daddy.'

'I have tried to deal with this, but Macbeth won't listen to me. Have you been in the hotel bar in the evenings?'

'No, what's going on?'

'The place is full every night with all the low life from Lochdubh.'

'Lochdubh doesn't have any low life.'

'Don't be deliberately obtuse. I'm talking about the men off the fishing boats and the forestry people.'

'What's up with them? You're a snob.'

'I'm a more practical businessman than I was when I started this venture,' said the colonel wearily. When he had run into debt, Hamish had suggested that he turn his family home into a hotel. The colonel had done this and the venture was successful, although he never gave Hamish any credit for having had the good idea in the first place. 'I'm not a snob,' said the colonel, 'but most of our guests are, and that you must admit. They come here to fish and shoot and play lords of the manor. They get dressed up to the nines in the evening. They go into the bar for a drink before dinner. The last thing they want is a lot of the local peasantry blocking off the heat from the fire. They even come in wearing wet clothes and steam in front of it like dogs. Have a word with Hamish Macbeth. He'll think of something.'

Priscilla decided to have a look at what the bar was like that evening before consulting Hamish. Most of the guests were English and not only did not smoke but, because they were middle-aged, had given up smoking at one time and had all the virulence of the reformed smoker. They were clustered at the bar, pointedly coughing and choking and waving their hands while the locals, grouped in front of the log fire, rolled cigarettes and lit them up, filling the air with pungent smoke. Priscilla realized her father was right. It was no use offending paying guests. They had a business to run.

On her way down to Lochdubh, she felt a little apprehensive at seeing Hamish again. They had been very close. It had been Hamish who had ended their relationship, becoming tired of Priscilla's ambitions to move him up to the CID in Strathbane and make him successful. Also she had never seemed to have any time for love-making. Why this was the case, Hamish had never been able to find out, and as for Priscilla, her mind clamped down tight shut on the subject.

She parked at the side of the police station and went round to the kitchen door. Hamish answered it and stood looking at her in surprise and then said, 'Come in, Priscilla. I heard you were back from London.'

Priscilla followed him into the narrow kitchen. Despite the warmth of the evening, Hamish had the wood-burning stove lit, a horrible old thing which Priscilla had once unsuccessfully tried to replace with a new electric cooker. There was an old-fashioned oil-lamp in the middle of the table. 'What's that for?' asked Priscilla. 'Has the electricity been cut off?'

'I like oil-lamps,' said Hamish. 'It saves on electricity and it gives a bonny light. Coffee? Or do you want a drink? I've got some whisky.'

'I don't want anything.' Priscilla sat down at the kitchen table and shrugged off her tweed jacket. Raindrops glistened in her fair hair. She looked as smooth, contained and elegant as ever. 'What I do want,' said Priscilla, 'is a bit of help, or rather, my father needs help.'

'Must be bad for the auld scunner to send you.'

'He's got a point, for once. The locals have given up the Lochdubh bar and are frequenting the hotel bar, smoking like chimneys, chattering away and hogging the fire. The guests are getting restless. We offer them elegant country house accommodation.'

'You'd think they would enjoy a bit of local colour.'

'Hamish, the fumes from their nasty cigarettes are so strong that they can hardly see anything, let alone local colour. What's the reason for it?'

'Have you been hearing about the Macho Man?'

'I've heard some great ape is enthralling the village with his adventures.'

'His name is Randy Duggan. He says he is American but becomes Scottish when he's drunk. He holds forth in the Lochdubh bar and the locals are beginning to find out that although he buys them a lot of drinks, they can't really get a chance to say much themselves. I merely suggested that if they moved up to the hotel bar for a wee bit, he might move on. That sort of person needs an audience.'

'Oh, Hamish, I might have guessed you were behind it. So why didn't this Randy just follow them to the hotel?'

'You've been away. Your father wouldnae let him stay at the hotel. So he took one of the holiday cottages up the back. Then there came these acts of vandalism. You heard of those?'

'Yes, and you suspect him?'

'Aye, but I havenae the proof.'

'So the problem remains. How do we get the locals out of the hotel?'

'I'll think o' something.'

The next day, Hamish made his way to the Lochdubh bar. It was empty of customers, not even Randy was there. The barman, a newcomer from Inverness, Pete Queen, was moodily polishing glasses.

'Quiet the day,' said Hamish.

'It'll be even mair quiet if the boss closes this place doon. Whit did I do wrong? The drinks here are cheaper than up at the castle.'

'Maybe they wanted a wee change,' said Hamish soothingly. 'It'll be easy enough to get them back.'

'How?'

'It's a good bit out o' the village, the hotel is, and they have to take their cars. I'll start checking them for drunk driving. Then if you were to have a happy hour, just for the one week, drinks at half price, they'd soon come back.'

Pete's narrow face brightened. 'I'll try anything. It's very good of you, Hamish. Have one on the house.'

'Too early for me,' said Hamish. 'Don't worry. Have you seen Duggan?'

'The big man? He was in here last night saying as how he was getting bored and he was thinking of moving on.'

'Let's hope he does.' Hamish sauntered out.

Hamish was no longer a favourite with the locals in the next two days. They found they were being breathalyzed in the hotel car park, their car keys taken away from them, and so they had to walk home and then were faced with the same long walk the next day to collect their cars. And outside the Lochdubh bar was a new sign advertising the happy hour. And so they were lured back.

But so was Randy Duggan, the Macho Man.

It was unfortunate for Geordie Mackenzie that while they had all been at the hotel, he had found new friends among the locals and an audience for *his* stories. He could not bear to sink back to obscurity. His resentment against Randy had been building up. The second evening after the locals had returned to the Lochdubh bar was a stormy one. Gales lashed rain against the steamed-up windows of the bar. The fishing boats would not be going out and so the bar was full.

Randy was bragging about how he had been a champion wrestler, when Geordie, who had drunk more than he was used to, piped up, 'I don't believe a word you say.'

His voice, although reedy, was perfectly clear and precise. Randy stopped in mid-sentence and glared at the retired schoolteacher. 'What did you say?' he roared. He was wearing a Stetson, pushed to the back of his head, and he flipped open the slats of his ridiculous glasses.

'I think you're a phoney,' said Geordie. 'That daft story about eating sheep's eyes. Every phoney who's been to the Middle East, or who pretends to have been in the Middle East, tells that story. It's a myth. It was a folk story which got around after a British army prank when some chap was told he had to eat sheep's eyes. No Arab actually eats them.'

Randy strutted over to Geordie. 'Are you calling me a liar?'

'Yes,' said Geordie, frightened but defiant.

'Then,' said Duggan with a nasty grin, 'it's time you cooled your head.'

He picked up Geordie by the scruff of the neck and carried him outside. Geordie kicked and wriggled and shouted for help. Everyone crowded outside the bar as Randy walked to the edge of the harbour and held the shrieking Geordie out over the water.

Hamish Macbeth came running up. 'Stop it. Stop it now!' he shouted.

Randy dropped Geordie contemptuously on to the quay and faced Hamish.

'You're a brave enough man when you're in uniform,' he sneered. 'You wouldn't dare stand up to me if you weren't a copper.'

Hamish looked at him with sudden hate. He loathed bullies. He knew how humiliated little Geordie was. He flared up. 'The day after tomorrow's my day off. I won't be in uniform then.'

'Then I'll meet you here after closing time at half past eleven at night,' said Randy, and sticking his thumbs in his belt, he strolled back into the bar. Hamish was cursing himself before he even reached the police station. Randy would make mincemeat of him. If word of it got back to Strathbane, he might lose his job, lose his cosy billet in the village. But he knew there was no way of getting out of the fight now.

The next day, the village was alive with gossip about the great fight to come and the gossip spread over the surrounding moorland and mountains to other towns and villages.

Bets were being laid, and most of them in favour of Duggan.

On the morning of the day of the fight, gloomy Hamish was beginning to wonder if he would still be alive at the end of it. Although he knew he had no feeling left for Priscilla, or so he told himself, he wanted to talk to someone about what a fool he had been, and Priscilla was the only person he could think of.

He found Priscilla in the gift shop. She was looking quite animated as she talked to a customer, a distinguished-looking middle-aged man. 'Morning, Hamish,' she said when she saw him. 'Let me introduce Mr John Glover to you. He's a banker from Glasgow who's staying at the hotel. Mr Glover, this is our local bobby.'

The two men shook hands. John Glover was tanned and handsome with thick black hair, greying a little at the sides. He was of medium height, impeccably groomed and tailored, making Hamish conscious that his uniform trousers were shiny and that his hair needed cutting. And to Hamish's dismay, he felt a stab of jealousy. 'I want to talk to you about something serious,' said Hamish.

But Priscilla looked reluctant to break off her conversation with John. 'Go to my rooms in the castle,' she said, 'and wait for me. I won't be long.'

Hamish slouched out moodily. In Priscilla's apartment at the top of the castle, he paced nervously up and down, and then, to take his mind off his troubles, he switched on the television set. Priscilla had satellite television. Hamish flicked the buttons on the remote control through pop singers and quiz shows, and then stopped and stared at the set in amazement, thinking he was looking at Duggan. It was a wrestling programme. There was the same figure, the same slatted glasses, the same fringed leather clothes and colourful hat. But the announcer was saying, 'And here is Randy Savage, the Macho Man, heavy-weight wrestling champion.'

Hamish leaned forward. Could it be the same man? But no, this one was better shaped, finer built, the only similarity was in the dress. Who, now, thought Hamish, had given Randy Duggan the nickname of the Macho Man? Surely Randy himself. He had said he had been a wrestler in America. Therefore it followed that he had taken the nickname and adopted the dress of one of America's wrestling heroes. But had he been a wrestler? Was anything he said true? Look how he claimed to be American and yet in his cups his accent thickened into a Scottish one, and a Lowland Scottish one at that.

His thoughts were interrupted by the arrival of Priscilla. He switched off the set. 'Well, Hamish,' she demanded briskly, 'what can I do for you?'

She was wearing a black wool dress with a white collar. Her hair was smooth and turned in at the ends. A shaft of sunlight shone on it.

'I've done something silly,' said Hamish. 'You know that fellow Randy Duggan we were talking about the other night?'

'The Macho Man. Yes, what about him?'

'Well, I've said I'll fight him tonight and I don't know if I'll come out of it alive.' He told her about the humiliation of Geordie, finishing with, 'It's a wonder you haven't heard about the fight. I'm sure everyone from here to Strathbane is laying bets on it.'

Priscilla's beautiful face hardened. 'Hamish, what is this? Policemen don't hold vulgar brawls with members of the public. Cancel it immediately!'

'I cannae. He would swagger about the village telling everyone what a coward I was.'

'Then on your own head be it. I'm sure that Highland brain of yours will find a way out of it. Fight dirty.'

'I haff my pride.'

'Your pride didn't stop you from going to bed with an elderly spinster, and a murderess at that!'

Priscilla was referring to a case where a Miss Gunnery had claimed to be in bed with Hamish in order to give him an alibi when he was a number-one suspect.

'She was only fifty and I didn't go to bed with her. I told you that.'

'Amazing how you went along with it.'

'I wasted my time coming here,' said Hamish crossly. 'I should have known better than to expect a bit o' womanly sympathy from you.' They glared at each other.

Then Hamish gave a reluctant laugh. 'It's a bit like old times, us quarrelling. Let's have dinner before the fight and talk about things.'

'I have a dinner date with John Glover.'

'That auld man!'

'Don't be silly. You're no spring chicken yourself. He's very charming.'

'Oh, suit yourself,' shouted Hamish, his face flaming as red as his hair. He strode out and crashed the door behind him.

He spent a miserable day, dreading the night to come. He had been in a few fights but never up against such a brute as Randy. He could already feel the big man's fists thudding into his face, bone cracking and blood spurting.

The gale had died down, but the rain fell steadily, fat drops running down the windows of the police station. Hamish sat by the stove in the kitchen, arms wrapped across his thin body for comfort, wishing, one way or another, it were all over.

But the clock on the kitchen wall ticked away the minutes and the hours and he could not think of any way of avoiding the fight.